The Substitute F

Max Marcin

Alpha Editions

This edition published in 2024

ISBN : 9789364736039

Design and Setting By
Alpha Editions
www.alphaedis.com
Email - info@alphaedis.com

As per information held with us this book is in Public Domain.
This book is a reproduction of an important historical work. Alpha Editions uses the best technology to reproduce historical work in the same manner it was first published to preserve its original nature. Any marks or number seen are left intentionally to preserve its true form.

Contents

CHAPTER I .... - 1 -

CHAPTER II .... - 9 -

CHAPTER III .... - 15 -

CHAPTER IV .... - 21 -

CHAPTER V .... - 24 -

CHAPTER VI .... - 34 -

CHAPTER VII .... - 47 -

CHAPTER VIII .... - 52 -

CHAPTER IX .... - 60 -

CHAPTER X .... - 69 -

CHAPTER XI .... - 74 -

CHAPTER XII .... - 84 -

CHAPTER XIII .... - 88 -

CHAPTER XIV .... - 94 -

CHAPTER XV .... - 100 -

CHAPTER XVI .... - 106 -

CHAPTER XVII	- 113 -
CHAPTER XVIII	- 122 -
CHAPTER XIX	- 127 -
CHAPTER XX	- 131 -
CHAPTER XXI	- 137 -
CHAPTER XXII	- 144 -
CHAPTER XXIII	- 149 -
CHAPTER XXIV	- 152 -

CHAPTER I

Did she come to threaten or to plead?

The question, darting swiftly through his mind as his eyes took in the unfamiliar outline of her figure, produced a storm of agitation which left him gazing stupidly at her, with fixed eyes in which surprise and terror mingled.

He had never seen her before—his first moment of survey impressed that clearly on him. Yet her presence in his home at this compromising hour signified that she was involved, remotely or intimately, in his own tangled affairs. The thought impelled him to closer scrutiny of her.

She was pleasing to the eye. But whether her beauty was soft and alluring or hard and repelling, his bewildered senses could not determine. Her toilet, fresh and elegant, rich and clinging, harmonizing with the velvet drapings and melting lights of the room, seemed to invest her with an air of breeding, gave her an outward show of refinement. Yet she betrayed certain signs of doubtful comfort, as if all this magnificence had been borrowed for the occasion.

He came forward noiselessly, his footsteps deadened in the soft pile of the Brussels carpet. She regarded his approach with cold, impassive demeanor, nodding slightly as he paused near the carved rosewood table above which hung an exquisitely wrought silver lamp, suspended by four silver chains from the ceiling.

"Mr. Herbert Whitmore?" she asked, not without trace of anxiety in her voice.

He observed that her skin had a warm and pearly tone, that her abundant hair was of a dark reddish tinge, and that her eyes, of turquoise blue, gleamed with a strange, impenetrable hue. He was still gazing vacantly at her, but his mind was working furiously, striving to answer the harrowing questions that presented themselves in tumultuous succession before it.

Who was she? What motive prompted this visit at ten in the evening? Did she come to plead a financial matter?—or was she here for purposes of blackmail? Did she have knowledge of his incriminating conduct, and was she sent to ensnare him into further complications? Above all, what attitude should he adopt toward her?

"What can I do for you?" he inquired in a tone frigidly polite, yet not devoid of an anxious note.

They regarded each other a moment.

"I hardly know how to begin," she said, lowering her eyes.

He did not credit her hesitancy. It was a deceit, he felt, a bit of theatricalism,—the simulated modesty of a woman of experience.

"Begin by being seated," he said rather sharply, as if he meant to convey that he penetrated her sham diffidence.

Ignoring his brusqueness, she dropped into one of the ornate rosewood chairs near the table.

"It is such a delicate matter on which I have come," she began timorously, eying him for a sign of encouragement. "Now that I am here I wish I hadn't come—it's so difficult for me to begin."

His keen gray eyes narrowed on her, but she read no encouragement in his glance. He had regained control of himself and assumed a non-committal attitude, as of one ready to listen, but indifferent as to whether she proceeded or withdrew.

"You haven't revealed the purpose of your visit as yet," he said, crossing his legs. "If you regret having come, you are at liberty to go without further explanation."

He hurled it at her as a challenge, but with a positive feeling that it would not be accepted.

"I have come to warn you," she said with sudden resolution.

"To warn me of what?" His brow knitted in puzzled surprise.

"I have come to tell you that he knows and has worked himself into a murderous fury."

"I don't understand." But his pretense of ignorance was too shallow not to be seen through immediately.

"You understand perfectly," she declared. "Moreover, you recognize your danger. It is useless to try to deceive me—an understanding between us might work to our mutual advantage."

He imagined that he perceived the sinister import of her suggestion. An understanding between them—that could mean only one thing. She had come to blackmail him.

"What sort of an understanding?" he asked experimentally.

She bent forward, thrusting her head directly underneath the overhanging lamp, revealing a face not untouched by care and suffering. He guessed her age at twenty-four, but the set earnestness of her expression made her seem close to thirty. She still possessed a certain girlishness, but it was marked and marred by an unpleasant maturity, as if she had arrived too young at a woman's understanding of the world. With physical beauty she was amply endowed; nor had it been hardened and coarsened beyond power to allure. There was no visible imperfection to detract from its charm; but, gazing on her, Whitmore felt something lacking, something spiritual, imponderable, yet immediately detected and missed. And this impression was heightened when she spoke.

"You are interested in George Collins and so am I," she said, and paused.

"And you've come to plead for him?" His manner signified that her errand was useless.

"Plead for him!" she echoed, a faint smile hovering about her lips. "Why should I plead for him with you? I came to tell you that he knows—and has bought a pistol."

"So he knows that I have learned of his conduct!" He studied the woman as if trying to read her inmost thoughts. "Does he suppose that by sending you with threats he can prevent me from telling—from telling—her?"

"He didn't send me," she retorted quickly. "I came without his knowledge. Nor do I care about what you have discovered! The point is that he has discovered that you have been urging his wife to divorce him. He accuses you of trying to disrupt his home. He is aware that you have been in correspondence with his wife and intends to intercept your next letter."

Whitmore's brow clouded. "Why did you come to tell me this?"

"For purely personal reasons."

"And who are you, madam?"

"I am——" She hesitated, as if afraid to disclose her identity. Then, overcoming her hesitancy, she said, "I am Julia Strong."

On hearing the name, the outward calm which he had maintained vanished, leaving him pale, agitated, apprehensive. Presently a mounting anger succeeded all other emotions, and he rose to his feet.

"What do you mean by coming here at this hour?" he demanded savagely. "You came here to warn me!—really, you overestimate my credulity!"

"I did come here to warn you," she persisted.

"And to betray George Collins!" The note of irony in his voice brought the blood to her cheeks.

"I don't want him to kill you," she said, controlling a clutch in her voice. "I want you to live. It is necessary—all my hopes and aspirations demand it."

He was on the point of making a sharp retort, but checked himself suddenly and regarded her with less aversion. Perhaps she was telling the truth! If so, the situation in which he found himself was not without its touch of grim humor. But what motive prompted her to extend the mantle of protection about him, and simultaneously to betray George Collins? He pondered the question a full minute. Then the simple solution, the only tenable one, occurred to him. She was ready to betray Collins for the same reason that had made her accept his protection.

"Madam," he said, with an eagerness he did not mean to betray, "knowing who you are, now I can guess at the nature of your hopes and aspirations. And you did right in coming to me. From what my detectives have communicated to me, I am led to believe that you are a woman with a keen appreciation of worldly comfort and luxury. I say this, without intending the slightest offense. You are aware, undoubtedly, that I am able to supply you with all you crave for—far in excess of anything that you can possibly hope to obtain from Collins. If you will consent to appear at my lawyer's office and make an affidavit——"

The changed expression on her face made him pause. She had risen and stood facing him, her eyes blazing resentment, her lips curled in a disdainful smile.

"I don't care to listen to your offensive utterances," she said, gazing at him as if to impale him with her glance. "I'm sorry I came. Good-night."

With an angry movement she donned her rich cloak, wrapping it about her figure and moving toward the door. He followed her with his eyes, until he saw her pass into the vestibule. Then he hastened forward and opened the street door.

She descended the broad steps holding herself stiffly erect, head uptilted—a striking figure, graceful, supple, almost commanding. In fact, so attractive was the picture she made as she stood a moment on the sidewalk, that a passing policeman, seized by a gallant impulse, opened the door of the waiting taxicab and held it ajar while she entered.

Balancing himself on the edge of the curb, the bluecoat stared after her in undisguised admiration until the cab swung around the corner; then he bestowed a curious glance on the house whence she had come. He saw that the door was half open and that a man's figure stood revealed in the soft light of the hallway. One hand was on the door knob, one foot was thrust forward as if the man were uncertain whether to plunge after her. Evidently he decided against venturing out, for he stepped back into the vestibule and shut the door.

"Even these people have their little scraps," the bluecoat murmured sagely, and passed on.

Herbert Whitmore did not return to the room in which he had received the visitor. Instead, he ascended the stairs to the library, and threw himself into the soft embrace of a wide leather chair.

The turmoil of his brain gave him an uncomfortable feeling of excitement, as if he were participating in something active and swift, which he but partly understood. He was incapable of connected thought—everything was vague and shadowy before him. In a dim way he recognized that he was standing in the way of an approaching avalanche, and gradually he began to discern the nature of the impending catastrophe. Presently the vague uncertainty that hovered before his mind resolved itself into action, and his groping forefinger pressed a button hidden beneath the carved edge of the library table. In response to the pressure, a liveried butler entered the room.

"Did you mail the letter I gave you?" inquired Whitmore.

"Yes, sir."

"When?"

"Immediately you gave it to me."

"That was about four hours ago?"

"Yes, sir."

"That is all."

The butler effaced himself from the room as noiselessly as he had entered, and again Whitmore gave himself up to the alarming predicament in which he found himself.

His reflections centered about the letter which the butler had mailed. It was not sent in a moment of impulsiveness. The information which it conveyed was not offered in spite, or in anger, or in envy. It was the deliberate act of a man habituated to clear thinking and correct action. Viewed with full knowledge of all the surrounding circumstances, that letter must be regarded as the noble outpouring of a chivalrous love, honest, worthy, unselfish. Regarded without the illumination of the complex conditions which called it forth, the letter was pregnant with possibility of mischief.

It was addressed to Mrs. George Collins. And George Collins must not be permitted to intercept it.

With the single resolve to frustrate Collins actuating his movements, Whitmore went to his apartment, slipped on his topcoat, and left the house. He paused at the corner to consult his watch. It was eleven o'clock.

He was sufficiently acquainted with the city to know that over on Seventh Avenue certain shops kept open until midnight. He had passed them frequently after theater and observed the industrious proprietors and barkers noisily soliciting trade on the sidewalk.

Down Fifth Avenue Whitmore swung at a rapid pace, turning west at Forty-second Street. Through the swirling crowds at Broadway he threaded his way, finally entering the gloomy thoroughfare that cuts a somber, murky streak through the illuminated area of Times Square.

Even Whitmore, engrossed as he was in his own affairs, could not help a feeling of depression as with a single step he emerged from the throbbing life and light of Broadway into the shabby darkness of Seventh Avenue. For nowhere in the big city is the contrast of its extremes brought home so sharply as at this intersection of three busy thoroughfares.

It is worth while to pause a moment in the blatant glare of that monstrously hideous variety house, that architectural malformation that defaces the northwest corner; or opposite in the shadow of the gray illumined tower that mounts undaunted, a connecting ladder between earth and sky. Especially profitable is it to pause a moment at the hour when the neighboring theaters are discharging their crowds, and to glance behind and beyond the furious activity that bewilders the eye and dazzles the senses. If you have the eye to see and the mind to appreciate, you will behold an illuminated canvas whereon is depicted, within the limited area of your vision, everything that a great city holds of wealth and poverty, beauty and ugliness, joy and sorrow, luxury and squalor, purity and degradation, truth and falsehood. It is all there, in this narrow environment, with the lights and the shadows meeting and blending, as the noise from below merges with the silence above.

Nothing of these vivid contrasts struck the sense of Whitmore as with nervous steps he hurried toward his destination. In the first place, familiarity with the scene had deprived him of the faculty to read its pitiless meaning; secondly, a feverish anxiety to have done with the business that dominated his mind and accelerated his footsteps sent him unheeding across Seventh Avenue and down that thoroughfare until he stopped abruptly before one of the shabby second-hand clothing stores with which the street abounds.

The air of prosperity with which he was invested saved him from being seized immediately by one of the bawling salesmen and dragged into the mothy interior of the shop. He was not of the type that submits to being manhandled and browbeaten into purchasing cast-off garments. But, as he stood hesitant and uncertain within the narrow radius of the gas-lit window, one of the barkers found sufficient courage to invite him within. And, to the utter amazement of the alert salesman, Whitmore entered the store.

The proprietor of the place, a stooped, be-whiskered man who spoke with a pronounced Hebraic accent, came forward to wait personally on this elegant customer. But he found that no especial skill was required to consummate a sale. Whitmore selected an old, dilapidated suit, a worn coat, an old slouch hat, and a pair of heavy shoes, and almost caused the beaming merchant to die of heart failure by paying the first price demanded of him.

"It's for an amateur theatrical performance," Whitmore explained to the proprietor, who was unable to hide his surprise that a customer of such seeming prosperity should invest in these cast-off garments.

With the bundle containing the clothes under his arm, Whitmore returned to Broadway and entered one of the hotels. He consulted a railroad time table, after which he called for a taxicab and directed the chauffeur to take him home.

He entered the house with his latchkey and climbed the stairs to his room. Divesting himself of coat and vest, he stepped before the mirror and shaved off his gray mustache. Next he produced a soft tennis shirt, which he exchanged for the linen one he had on, and an old bow tie took the place of the blue four-in-hand which he usually wore.

Undoing the bundle with which he had entered the house, he proceeded to dress in the second-hand garments. When he had pulled the battered slouch hat well down on his forehead, he surveyed himself in the glass. The transformation was complete.

Regarding himself in this shabby disguise, he almost deteriorated in his own estimation. It was difficult to believe that a mere change of apparel could make such a vast difference. But one satisfaction he could not deny himself. It was unlikely that anyone would recognize, in the human derelict before the looking-glass, Herbert Whitmore, millionaire, owner of the great Whitmore Iron Works. It was certain that his most intimate friend would have failed to penetrate his disguise.

Dismissing the unpleasant reflections kindled within him, Whitmore proceeded with characteristic assurance to execute what was in his mind. He descended silently to the basement of the house, where he obtained a heavy screw-driver. This he secreted in the inside pocket of his coat. Next he went to the basement door and peered furtively through the grating. His anxious eyes swept the street until convinced that no inquisitive policeman was loitering in the immediate vicinity. Then, slowly, apprehensively, he opened the door and issued, like a thief in the night, from his own home.

CHAPTER II

The domestic life of George Collins and his wife was a daily lie which fooled no one. For five years they had lived completely estranged beneath the single roof that sheltered both, yet trying desperately to conceal their conjugal infelicity from the world. But the eyes of the world are too keen and penetrating when it comes to other people's affairs, and such painful efforts as the Collinses made to appear reconciled to each other were measured and appraised at their true worth.

Marriage is a common institution and the symptoms of its discontent are familiar to all. They appeared early in the married life of the Collinses, were faithfully diagnosed by the members of their immediate circle, and the prognostication based on them called for the early appearance of Mrs. Collins as plaintiff in the divorce court.

But religious scruples and a natural abhorrence of such a proceeding combined to keep the wife from making the one essential move necessary for her freedom.

Rather than do violence to the tenets of her religious faith and to the rigid principles of her upbringing, she chose to bear the burden of unhappiness that was imposed on her. Occasionally she and her husband even appeared in public together, and on such occasions they tried to give the impression of entertaining for each other all the affection of a happily married couple. But in their own home they lived continuously in a state of mutual aversion and estrangement, occupying separate apartments and holding only the most formal communications with each other.

The house which they occupied was a stately stucco structure, situated on top of a terraced lawn and approached by a gravel walk banked with flowers and shrubs. A sloping roof, painted a dull red and pierced by a huge chimney, gave a warm and picturesque tone to the place, which otherwise might have appeared coldly severe and uninviting.

The luxurious seclusion which the Collinses enjoyed was shared by about sixty neighbors who formed the wealthy colony of Delmore Park, a small suburb within easy motoring and commuting distance of New York. The park itself was an attractive inclosure of some three hundred acres, surrounded by a fence of high iron palings and laid out so as to give the impression from within of a natural forest, while, as a matter of fact, the place was a triumph of the consummate skill of expert gardeners. In this deliberately fashioned woodland it was possible to combine all the pomp and extravagance of city life with the rustic attractiveness and simplicity of the country—a combination toward which the wealthy are turning in increasing numbers each year.

On the morning following Whitmore's strange nocturnal excursion, Collins's alarm clock set up an ear-splitting din at a most unwonted hour. On retiring the previous night Collins had set the alarm for seven-thirty, an hour at which he usually attained his deepest sleep. Only on rare occasions was he known to retire before two A. M., and still rarer were the occasions when he relinquished his bed before eleven.

A product of the gay night life of the city, he required the mornings for slumber. Nor did he on this particular morning rouse himself into immediate activity. Stretching himself languorously, he permitted the alarm to exhaust itself, then buried his head in his pillow.

But he did not close his eyes. With a painful effort he prevented his tired eyelids from falling and for half an hour remained stretched between the sheets, lost in gloomy reflection.

There had been a purpose in setting the alarm at this early hour; the same purpose now held him awake, absorbed in thought, yet alert to every sound about the house. He heard the butler unlock the storm doors and the servants prepare for the morning work. An occasional delivery wagon ground through the gravel walk, the grating noise of the wheels rasping his quivering nerves.

Through the open window a stream of sunshine flooded the floor and distributed itself impartially about the room. The fresh arena of spring blossoms softened the crisp morning air with a pleasant perfume; feathered throats chirped happily in pursuit of the early worm.

The swelling chorus of happiness without aroused no responsive quiver in Collins's heart. It hung within him, a leaden weight coiled with bitterness and hate. His mind was a blazing furnace of furious resentment, emitting sparks of rage that kindled other fires in the storehouse of his emotions, until his temper seemed to reflect the conflict of all tempers.

The shrill call of a letter-carrier's whistle banished the silent fury into which he had worked himself. A thrill of expectancy shot down his frame. Donning his bathrobe and slippers he stepped into the hallway and listened. The butler and the mail man exchanged a word of greeting, then the former closed the door. Collins descended the stairs, blinking, with sleepy dissipated eyes.

"Give me all the mail," he said, extending a tremulous hand.

"There's a letter for madam—"

"Give it to me!"

Reluctantly the butler delivered the letter to him.

"You needn't mention my having received all the mail," Collins growled. "If madam asks whether there was any mail for her tell her there wasn't any. And don't forget what I say!"

The butler stared after him as he climbed up the stairs and disappeared into his own room.

Seated on the edge of his bed, Collins glanced through his personal mail then tore open the letter to his wife. It was in a familiar handwriting and the contents brought no look of surprise to his face. But he read it through half a dozen times, as if to sear it into his memory.

Presently he dressed and went out for a stroll, drinking copious draughts of the bracing morning air. But the tormenting presence of the intercepted letter in his pocket drew him back to the house. He encountered his wife in the hallway.

"There was some mail for me—where is it?" she said, extending a hand confidently.

He produced the letter from his pocket, poising it tantalizingly between his fingers. She recognized the handwriting and a wave of red mounted to her forehead. Also, she observed the ragged slit at the top of the envelope and the painful realization that he had read the contents rushed on her.

"How dared you?" She tried to seize the letter, but he, anticipating her move, withdrew his arm and thrust the missive into his pocket. "I didn't believe it possible you could sink so low," she murmured. "But this is the end," she added with sudden vehemence. "I shall leave this house to-day."

"Oh, no, you won't!" An angry scowl contorted his face. "You've flaunted your superior virtues in my face—accused me of cruelty and neglect and selfishness. Everybody, including your brother, believes you to be the long-suffering, patient little angel. You've been the woman with the noble soul— I've been the unworthy rascal. Now you stand there, your feelings outraged, because I had the foresight to intercept an incriminating letter. You calmly tell me it's the end. You're going to leave. It makes no difference how much scandal you bring on my name. You—"

She checked him with a contemptuous toss of the head. All the suffering which she had endured through the years of their married life now resolved itself into a fury of resentment.

"Your name!" she exclaimed with cutting irony. "As if anything which I might do could add to the weight of dishonor that you have imposed upon it! I don't know the contents of that letter, but it's from Herbert Whitmore and he's as incapable of a dishonorable act as you are incapable of anything honorable. And you had the audacity to open and read that letter!"

She paused, fixing him with her eyes, her lips curled into a disdainful smile. But the fire of her scorn left him unseared. His calloused sensibilities had long ago lost their capability of appreciating a nature such as hers. For his wife to have a letter addressed to her such as he had intercepted, spelled guilt. The debasing environment into which he had plunged on inheriting the fortune which his father had accumulated, had undermined all his faith in womanhood. He could not see beyond the Tenderloin purview.

But pride and selfishness were screamingly alive within him. To these was added the inordinate conceit of the habitual libertine, a combination than which there is nothing more sensitive in the entire human composition.

But as Collins gazed on the graceful lines of her full figure and on the almost classic beauty of her marmoreal features, he could not stifle a pang of anxiety at thought of losing her. The fact that he had discarded her in all but name, for the dubious pleasures of a life of dissipation, did not occur to him. He believed in the established moral code that excuses the offenses of the man and eternally condemns the woman. Yet, ready as he was to attribute culpability to her conduct, it was hard even for him to reconcile her smooth, artless brow, her frank, limpid eyes, her delicate, sensitive lips, with any act that savored of unworthiness or deceit.

"It's hard to look at you and believe you guilty of wrong," he said resentfully.

"It makes no difference to me what you believe," she snapped. "I'm through with you! I shall obtain a divorce."

The storm which had been gathering force within him all morning now broke in all its fury.

"You're going to get a divorce!" he cried ironically. "You still pretend to be the injured one. You and Whitmore have it all framed up—eh! But I tell you you've miscalculated this time! No man can wreck my home with impunity! No man can enter my house to steal my wife—and get away with it. I've been blind a long time, but my eyes are wide open now."

He walked to the telephone at the rear of the hall and lifted the receiver off the hook.

"What are you going to do?" she demanded.

"Call up your brother. We'll see what he has to say about it."

Lester Ward, the brother of Mrs. Collins, also lived in Delmore Park. He had succeeded to his father's banking business and occupied the house which his parents had left. Fifteen minutes after Collins summoned him over the telephone, he was seated in his sister's library, prepared to mediate in what he guessed to be another quarrel between her and her husband.

"This letter will explain itself," Collins opened the conversation. Lifting the note out of the envelope, he read:

"*My Dear Grace*:

"Since I communicated with you last, additional reasons have developed to justify your leaving him immediately. Your belief that with all his faults he has adhered to his marriage vows is but a delusion born of your own pure nature. I have the proof, if you care to hear it. Grace, you told me you loved me. My love for you is undiminished. Why sacrifice yourself longer—why sacrifice me? I cannot endure to be parted from you. Start for Reno at once—to-morrow is not too soon. Our love is too holy to be smitten and made to suffer by one entirely unworthy of your slightest consideration. Leave him, Grace, and come to me.

"Yours devotedly,
HERBERT."

"Well, what do you think of that?" Collins asked, turning toward his brother-in-law. "My wife loves another man. And he's urging her to wreck her home!"

Ward's eyes alternated between his sister and her husband.

"Of course, she's not going to do it," he said as if expressing an inevitable conclusion.

"I'm going to leave here this very day," she declared firmly.

"And plunge into the scandal of a divorce proceeding?" Her brother bestowed a reproachful glance upon her. "Grace, you know how I feel toward your husband. Long ago I urged you to divorce him, but you refused. Now you must consider me. Think of the notoriety! My approaching marriage must not be overcast by the awful scandal that will follow your trip to Reno. Were we less prominent socially, it might be different. But the newspapers will be full of it. No, Grace, don't do anything hasty—not just now."

"You counsel me to continue living with him?" she inquired.

"I simply ask you to continue as you're doing."

She bent forward in her chair, her face set in an expression of unalterable determination.

"I love Herbert," she declared calmly, unmindful of the amazement which her avowal produced. "I have loved him a long while," she continued undismayed. "I crave him—I loathe the man to whom I am wedded."

"I sympathize with you," the brother hastened to assure her, "and, were it not for my marriage, I should urge you to leave him at once. He's a cad—"

"I'm not the sort of cad that permits another man to destroy his home," blurted Collins.

The others ignored his interruption.

"Lester," said the wife, "I shall leave this house to-day. Regardless of your marriage, I shall apply for a divorce and marry Herbert Whitmore."

The strained silence which followed was broken by Collins. He arose and walked to the door.

"You'll never marry Whitmore," he said. "There is a higher law that protects the home."

"Why—what do you mean?" the wife inquired in a tone of alarm. Something in her husband's face, something she had never seen there before, frightened her.

"I'm going to kill Whitmore," he said, leaving the room.

CHAPTER III

A premeditated killing wherein the murderer makes no provision to protect himself from the sure consequences of his act, requires a certain amount of perverted courage. Neither Mrs. Collins nor her brother credited Collins with the possession of even this low courage—at least not in sufficient degree to induce him to relinquish the comforts of freedom for the inconveniences of a prison. So they offered no objection to his departure, permitting him to leave without a word, as though they were entirely unconcerned in what he did.

Knowing Collins intimately as they did, it was impossible to take his assumption of the rôle of an outraged husband seriously. They saw, only too clearly, the ridiculous figure he made in the false light with which he had invested himself. But when he was gone, with his threat still echoing through their brains, they began to doubt their first impression of his cowardice.

"That's a fine mess you've made of it," said Ward, who had grown palpably uneasy.

"I made the mess when I married him," replied the sister. "I shall now proceed to disentangle myself from it. Until I start for Reno I shall live at your house."

"You don't think, really, that he would shoot?" The brother's face expressed incredulity, mixed with worry.

Her forehead contracted in thought.

"As he is now, I feel certain he would not dare. But should he start drinking—"

Ward was on his feet, his pale face grown paler.

"That's just it!" he exclaimed. "We must forestall him."

The same thought had flashed through her brain and she was already on the way to the telephone. She called up Whitmore's house and asked for the merchant.

"He didn't come home last night," the butler informed her.

Although burning with anxiety she made no further inquiries of the servant. Instead, she rang up Whitmore's office.

"No ma'am, he hasn't been here this morning," the office boy said.

"Then give me Mr. Beard, his secretary."

"He hasn't been here, either."

She hung up the receiver and turned a bewildered countenance to her brother.

"There is something singular about Herbert's absence from home and his failure to appear at the office," she said. "I don't know why I should think so—but I do."

"It's impossible for your husband to have reached the city," Ward answered reassuringly. "He won't get there for twenty-five minutes and the chances are he'll stop in various saloons before he tries to find Whitmore. I'll have my car here in ten minutes and we'll proceed at once to Whitmore's office and wait for him. Now hurry and get dressed."

Ward paced the drawing-room while waiting for his sister to finish her toilet. He had telephoned for his automobile and heard the car draw up at the gate. In the presence of Mrs. Collins and her husband, Ward had maintained an unruffled demeanor; now that he was alone his face assumed a tense, rigid look, as though he were staring at an apparition. Something weighed heavily on his mind and it was plain that he was beset by uncertainty. He continued to walk up and down the room with short, nervous strides, until the swish of skirts at the head of the stairs brought him to an abrupt halt at the doorway. The arm which he extended to his sister, as he escorted her to the waiting automobile trembled violently. A cold sweat moistened his face.

"Sis," he said, when the machine had started, "I'm going to tell you something. Things are headed for a great crisis and it is necessary that you should know. It's going to shock you—"

He paused, eyeing her quizzically. But her mind, occupied with the safety of the man she loved, understood but vaguely what he was saying.

The brother took advantage of her preoccupation to gather additional courage for the communication which he had to impart. He saw clearly that she was resolved to discard her husband, that it would be futile to combat her determination. Other occasions there had been, many of them, when he had averted a final parting between them. But there had never been another man involved.

"Grace, listen to me!" He placed one hand on her wrist. "We are both in a terrible predicament, out of which my marriage may lift us. If you do anything that endangers the marriage, if my engagement should be broken,—we are both ruined."

"What do you mean?" A puzzled look appeared in her face.

"I didn't tell you before, because I thought it would never be necessary to do so," he went on, growing more nervous and uneasy. "But little by little I put all our money into the South American Developing Company which I promoted, and the enterprise is a failure. Moreover, I induced most of the clients of the bank to invest—I grow sick every time I contemplate what's going to happen when they learn that their money is lost. But there was nothing dishonest, sis—nothing dishonest!"

The news appeared to have no visible effect upon her. Something more important than money, more alarming than the ruin which his words implied, distracted her with a vague foreboding of impending evil. She made no reply to her brother, but sat rigid, eyes staring vacantly ahead, her hands tightly clasped beneath the heavy fur rug that protected the lower part of her body.

The automobile sped on, smoothly as though running on steel rails. A brisk wind beat against the glass shield and was deflected, leaving only light currents of air to brush the faces of the occupants of the car. Between Ward and his sister a long silence ensued.

It was broken by the brother.

"Don't you understand the position we're in?" he inquired.

"I understand," she replied absently.

"And don't you care?"

"Nothing matters now, except Herbert."

For weeks the brother had dreaded the moment when he should be compelled to confess the loss of their fortune. Now, finding that she took it coolly, even indifferently, he decided to go through with it.

"But I haven't finished—you don't know all," he pursued desperately. "The situation is aggravated by your resolve to leave your husband. All his money, save the small income from the trust fund established by his mother, is likewise sunk in the enterprise. I induced him to invest, I'm really responsible for the predicament in which he'll find himself. Don't you see," he added pleadingly, "if you leave him now it will take on the aspect of desertion. People will say that your brother ruined him and then you threw him over. While if you wait until after my marriage, I shall be in a position to settle with him in full and still have enough to look after you."

For several minutes she remained mute, evidently digesting his words.

"And would you marry without letting her know that you are ruined?" she inquired in quivering tones. "Would you try to rehabilitate yourself with her fortune? Do you think it fair?"

The words cut like saber thrusts. But when a man finds the walls of his house about to fall on him he is apt to clutch blindly at anything which promises to prop the tottering structure.

"It is cowardly, I confess," he said. "But what am I to do? Besides, I love her. You know I would not marry without love, even to avert financial ruin."

"I shall not interfere between you and your intended," she answered icily. "Neither shall I permit the circumstances which you have described to alter my determination."

The car now threaded its way through the maze of traffic in the city. Presently it drew up before a huge, ugly factory that covered a square block on the upper west side, near the river. Ward and his sister jumped out of the tonneau and entered the building. They found themselves in a busy office, consisting of a single room down the length of which a wooden rail interposed between visitors and employés.

"I wish to see Mr. Whitmore," Mrs. Collins informed one of the office boys.

"Hasn't come down yet," the boy replied.

"Is he often away as late as this?"

"No ma'am," said the boy. "He's usually here at nine o'clock."

"Has Mr. Beard been here this morning?"

"Not yet. But he telephoned he'll be here at twelve o'clock."

Ward consulted his watch. It was a quarter past ten. He questioned the boy but was unable to obtain any information as to the possible whereabouts of his employer or his secretary. So he and his sister decided to await them at the office.

The visitors looked sufficiently important to warrant the office boy ushering them into Whitmore's private office. As they passed down the railed corridor they elicited the further information that no one answering Collins's description had called that morning.

"He's probably patronizing a bar somewhere between here and the Grand Central Station just now," commented Ward in an undertone.

They did not enter into further discussion of their impending financial ruin while awaiting Whitmore. Immediately on dropping into a chair Mrs. Collins seemed to draw within herself, surrendering to the harrowing thoughts that filled her mind. Ward also became deeply preoccupied with his own tangled affairs, his brain striving furiously to find some solution of the dilemma into which he was plunged.

They took no note of the passing time; but the minutes sped swiftly while they wrestled silently with the problems that had entered their lives and when Ward suddenly looked up the hands of the little brass clock on top of Whitmore's desk pointed to a quarter of twelve. An instant later the door of the office was flung open and a tall figure, clean-shaven, with clearly defined features, burst into the room.

On seeing the visitors the man paused, perplexed. It was plain that he was under great stress of mind. His face was haggard, his eyes were sunken, his mouth drawn, as if he had not yet recovered from some great shock.

"Ward—Mrs. Collins!" he stammered.

The voice recalled the woman out of the dreamy state into which she had lapsed. She scrutinized the man with eyes in which terror and suspense mingled.

"Mr. Beard—why!—something has happened!" she gave voice to her fear.

"Yes, something dreadful has occurred," he said, trying to avert his face.

A great fear shook the woman's frame. For an instant she raised her eyes imploringly, then lowered them.

"Then he has killed him—murdered him?" The words came as though each syllable wrenched her heart.

"Killed him?" repeated Beard with rising inflection. "Why, what do you mean?"

"My husband—Mr. Collins—he set out this morning to do it. For God's sake," she implored, "don't keep me in suspense. Tell me what happened."

By a violent effort Beard recovered sufficient calm to note the agitation of the woman.

"Why, no," he said reassuringly, "Mr. Whitmore hasn't been killed."

"But what has happened?" demanded Mrs. Collins with a gesture of impatience.

"I cannot tell you," answered the secretary. "But something has occurred—a grave crisis has arisen in Mr. Whitmore's life. He will not be at his office for some time—perhaps not for weeks, or months, or years. But he asked me to communicate with you, to let you know that he will notify you the moment he returns. Meanwhile, he asks you to believe in him, even though he cannot write to you. More than that I cannot tell you."

Ward and his sister exchanged bewildered glances. The unexpected turn of events left them speechless. And, before they were able to recover their dazed senses, Beard slipped out of the office and lost himself among the small army of clerks and bookkeepers in the outer room.

Ward, finally observing that he was alone with his sister, bestowed on her a bitter smile.

"What a muddle!" he exclaimed. "Domestic trouble ... financial difficulties!... Whitmore vanished! What next?"

She stared at him through swimming eyes. Her lips moved but no sound came from them.

"Take the car home, Grace," he said in milder voice. "I'll go to the office and try to puzzle this thing out."

CHAPTER IV

What had become of Herbert Whitmore?

Like a thief in the night he had slipped out of his Fifth Avenue home, disappeared from his business, vanished like a specter, while the domestic tragedy of the Collinses paused in anticipation of his reappearance.

Beard, the confidential secretary, had taken possession of his employer's office, and to all inquiries regarding Whitmore's absence, made the same reply:

"He is gone indefinitely on a business trip."

Not even the persistent Collins was able to elicit anything additional. No further information was vouchsafed Mrs. Collins, who had taken up her abode with her brother; the financially troubled Ward, desperately fighting off ruin, could learn nothing from the silent, inscrutable Beard.

Then, one morning, unostentatiously as he had disappeared, Whitmore returned to his office. He wore a new spring coat, a new soft hat, new gloves and shoes, an unfamiliar brown tie against a striped shirt-bosom, as if he had just stepped out of a haberdasher's shop.

Down the long aisle, between the two rows of desks he passed, nodding with that air of pleasant kindliness that had endeared him to his hundreds of employés.

"Good morning, Mr. Whitmore—glad to see you back!" was fired at him with respectful familiarity from a score of clerks.

He smiled amiably, replying occasionally with a cheery rejoinder. Evidently he was in excellent spirits.

Whitmore's private office, at the rear of the long hall, ran the full width of the room. It was partitioned off from the main room by a glass partition through which he was at all times visible to his employés. The office contained no windows, being shut in on three sides by the thick walls of the building, and obtained its light through the glass paneling of the partition. The floor was covered by a green carpet and three or four chairs rested against the wall.

"Sam!" the merchant called to his office boy. "I shall be very busy with my papers this morning. Permit no one to enter my office and don't bring any visitors' cards."

Whitmore placed his hand affectionately on the boy's tousled hair.

"Don't forget my instructions!" he said pleasantly.

The merchant permitted the glass door of his office to remain open. Divesting himself of his coat he dropped into the revolving chair at his desk and swung around so as to sit with his back toward the outer office.

Behind the transparent partition he worked, sorting papers and slipping them into pigeon-holes. Toward noon one of the clerks observed that the merchant had slipped down into his chair, that his head hung strangely to one side.

"What's the matter with Mr. Whitmore?" the clerk asked the office boy.

The two thrust their faces against the intervening glass, noting that the employer's limbs were rigidly outstretched and that one hand hung limply at his side while the other rested on the desk.

They tiptoed into the office, like guilty schoolboys bent on eavesdropping. A single glance at Whitmore's white face and they burst through the door, their faces distorted with terror.

"Something's happened to Mr. Whitmore!" shouted the clerk.

Drummond, the head clerk, leaped forward in a quick offer of assistance. He remained a minute or two in the private office, then emerged, haggard, with eyes staring.

"Mr. Whitmore's been shot!" burst from his lips. "Get a policeman. He's dead," he added with a sob.

The news seemed to strike the office dumb. The clerks regarded each other like bewildered sheep, awed, terrified, a vague fear gripping their hearts. In the midst of their furious, living activity, the specter of death had suddenly appeared. It had crept in on them silently, stealthily, selecting the most shining mark as its victim. Unannounced, it had proclaimed the frailty of human life more effectively than if it had revealed itself in a lightning bolt. With noiseless, unseen hands, it had abducted the most beloved figure among them, deprived them forever of the kindly, fatherly personality of the man whom they had come to regard more as a friend than an employer.

Recovering from their first terror, the clerks left their desks and massed forward toward the partition, but the head clerk waved them back.

"Everyone remain in his place until after the police have arrived," he ordered.

The office boy, who had gone to summon a policeman, now returned with the bluecoat. The latter examined the dead man an instant, then, following the usual custom, summoned an ambulance and notified the coroner.

"Looks like a suicide," he declared over the telephone.

The ambulance was the first to arrive and the young surgeon, after listening vainly for a promising flutter of the heart, officially pronounced the merchant dead. When the coroner arrived, he was assured that nothing in the private office had been disturbed, after which he proceeded with his investigation.

Almost the first object which he noticed was a shiny revolver lying on the desk, about an inch from the dead man's fingers. As he lifted the weapon, he observed that the merchant had been shot in the side, and, turning toward the policeman, said:

"A plain case of suicide."

More as a matter of form, rather than with any hope of discovering anything of value, the coroner opened the revolver, and, as he did so, an exclamation of surprise escaped his lips. His eyes fixed themselves on the loaded chambers of the barrel in a puzzled stare until he was convinced that his senses were not deceiving him.

The revolver was fully loaded. It had never been fired.

Switching on the electric lights, the coroner examined the clothing of the victim. There were no powder marks where the bullet had entered.

"Officer, this is murder!" he exclaimed excitedly. "Notify the detective bureau. And don't permit anyone to leave this building."

CHAPTER V

While awaiting the arrival of the Headquarters men, the coroner busied himself with a preliminary examination of the clerks. The coroner was a small, fussy individual, smooth-shaven, with reddish-brown hair brushed back in pompadour fashion. Because of his small stature and insignificant appearance he was compelled to adopt a brisk air of command, lest witnesses presume to trifle with his authority.

"Gentlemen, I am Coroner Hart," he announced, stepping into the outer office and addressing the assembled clerks. "I shall immediately begin a preliminary inquest and you will all regard yourselves summoned as witnesses. The policeman will permit no one to leave the room without my permission."

The clerks, unfamiliar with the legal proceedings attached to a homicide case, exchanged puzzled glances. In the presence of their beloved dead, this man's unsympathetic attitude seemed almost a profanation. The policeman, in passing through the office on his way to the door, had let drop the remark that murder had been committed, yet none of the employés could bring himself to believe that an alien hand had fired the mortal bullet. No visitor had entered Whitmore's office; none of the clerks had been within. Who could have done it?

The coroner called one of the clerks who had sat within a dozen feet of the door all morning.

"Did you see anyone enter the office?" he asked.

"No, sir," the clerk replied.

"Could anyone have entered without passing you or without your noticing him?"

"Absolutely not."

"Did you hear the shot fired?"

"I didn't hear a sound after Mr. Whitmore entered the office."

"And your hearing—is it good?"

"Perfect."

After putting the same questions to half a dozen other clerks and obtaining similar answers, Coroner Hart decided to save time by addressing himself to the employés in general.

"If anyone saw any person enter that office this morning or heard a shot, let him come forward," he called.

The men stood mute, eyeing one another expectantly, each hoping someone else might have valuable information to offer. The hush finally was broken by a shuffling of feet as two strangers thrust their way through the crowd and ranged themselves on either side of the coroner.

One of the newcomers, the less heavily built of the two, compelled immediate attention by reason of his personality. He carried himself with an air of certainty, as if accustomed to meeting grave problems—and solving them. As he stood at the right of the coroner, his keen gray eyes, set deep beneath the arched outline of his eyebrows, swept the faces of the sorrowing employés, as if trying to read their inmost thoughts. Despite the severe cast of his features, there was something engaging about the man, some magic of personality, that drew one irresistibly toward him.

"Just in time to hear the most important witness," the coroner said to him, at the same time beckoning the office boy to come forward.

The two visitors and the coroner seated themselves at one of the flat-top desks, while the boy, pale, trembling, as if conscious of some guilty act, faced them with fear written in his youthful countenance. The coroner solemnly administered the customary oath.

"You know what will happen to you if you tell a lie?" he asked.

"Yes, sir, I'll be sent to prison," the boy answered timorously.

"Now what is your name?"

"Samuel Johnson."

The witness further confided that he had been employed in the establishment three years, that he had seen Mr. Whitmore enter the office and that thereafter he had occupied a seat within a foot of the door until one of the clerks called his attention to the peculiar attitude in which his employer had fallen in the chair.

"What did Mr. Whitmore say to you when he arrived this morning?" inquired the coroner.

"He'd been away for six weeks, and he put his hand on my head like he was glad to see me and said that no one was to be admitted to the office and I wasn't to bring in any visitor's card." The boy sobbed convulsively as he recalled the last words of his employer.

"Were any visitors here this morning?"

"No, sir."

"Did any of the clerks enter the office?"

"No, sir."

"Did you hear a shot fired, or any other peculiar sound?"

"I did not."

"Are you positive?"

"I hope I may die on the spot if it ain't so," the witness said fervently.

The coroner's eyes alternated between his two visitors. The smaller of the two devoted himself to a long scrutiny of the boy's countenance.

"Mr. Whitmore was absent for six weeks?" he suddenly asked.

"Yes, sir."

"Do you know where he was?"

"Mr. Beard told me to tell all visitors that Mr. Whitmore was away on a business trip."

"Who is Mr. Beard?"

"Mr. Whitmore's confidential secretary. He took charge of the business while Mr. Whitmore was away."

"Isn't it somewhat unusual that nobody called to see Mr. Whitmore on his return this morning?"

"I guess they didn't know he was back," the boy replied.

"Did Mr. Whitmore have any trouble with anyone before he left?"

"Not that I know of. But after he was gone a man came around here every day for four weeks looking for him. The man looked like a Broadway dude—like he drank a whole lot and didn't sleep much. I once heard him tell Mr. Beard that Mr. Whitmore had run away from him."

The coroner and the visitors exchanged meaning glances.

"Where is Mr. Beard?" inquired the coroner.

"He didn't come down to-day."

Again the coroner looked gravely at the others, but their faces failed to indicate what import they attached to the boy's statements.

"Lieutenant, is there any other question you desire to ask?"

"No, coroner, I think we'd better adjourn to the private office," said the man addressed.

Entering the merchant's office, the coroner closed the door behind them.

"Lieutenant Britz," he remarked cordially, "I'm glad they sent you up. This looks like a mystery worthy of your talents."

Lieutenant Britz disregarded the implied compliment. He had taken up a position of survey in the center of the room, from which his eyes traveled slowly about the place, studying every inch of the carpet, lingering on the black leather surface of the chairs, covering the wide area of the walls.

"Have you searched the body?" he asked.

"Yes," replied the coroner. "Only a key ring with four keys attached was found in the pockets."

"How about the papers in the desk?"

"Nothing but business papers."

At this juncture a clerk poked his head timidly into the room and said:

"Officers, it's three o'clock now and we haven't been out to lunch. May we go?"

"I'll let you know in a minute or two," answered the coroner. When the clerk had withdrawn his head, the official stepped over to Britz.

"Those clerks are in a conspiracy of silence," he declared. "This man could not have committed suicide. The pistol found on the desk was fully loaded. The clothing is devoid of powder stains. Moreover, a most careful search has failed to reveal any other weapon. Now, someone entered this room and fired the shot. Yet all those clerks maintain that no one has been in here and that they heard no shot, although the door stood open all the while the merchant was in the office. Somebody has secreted the pistol with which the shooting was done and it might be well to search all the clerks."

"That would be a useless procedure," replied Britz. "There is no conspiracy of silence. If those men outside could shed any light on the crime, they would do so eagerly. The murderer could not have enjoined silence on thirty or thirty-five men. No, they have told all they know. You may permit them to enjoy their lunch."

Although the coroner was the ranking official, his respect for Britz's judgment was such that he invariably followed the latter's suggestions. So he informed the clerks they could leave the building at will.

While the coroner was in the big room addressing the employés, Britz suddenly walked to the chair in which the murdered man still sat huddled. Bending down, he picked up something long and shiny, which the others had overlooked. It was a long darning needle, and the detective, after examining it an instant under the electric light, slipped it into a leather card case. He did not mention what he had found to the coroner, when the latter returned.

"Greig," said Britz to his bulky companion, "go out and fetch a step-ladder. Let us examine the walls and ceiling."

Greig hastened out of the office, returning in a few minutes with the ladder. The two detectives devoted half an hour to sounding the walls and ceiling, while the coroner wrote out the necessary permit for the removal of the body.

"Everything is absolutely solid," declared Britz, when he had finished his examination. "There are no panels in the wall through which the assassin might have entered."

"That's what I thought," beamed the coroner. "The murderer entered and left through the door. And some of those clerks, if not all of them, must have seen him—or her. I tell you they're in a conspiracy to shield the murderer."

Britz extended a hand toward the glass partition.

"Look down this room," he said. "The murderer, presuming it was a man, must have passed down this long aisle into the office. Then, it was necessary to repeat the journey in order to escape. Had there been a conspiracy, then those thirty clerks must have remained quietly at their desks while the assassin walked out of the room. Do you believe these men would have permitted him to escape?"

"Suppose he carried the pistol in his hand, don't you believe he could have intimidated them?" ventured Greig.

"Sure!" joined the coroner. "And the men may now be ashamed of their cowardice."

"That wouldn't have prevented them giving the alarm after the murderer left," declared Britz. "No, coroner, no one saw the slayer enter or leave. In fact, he did not enter through the door."

"Then how did he get in?" demanded the coroner. "Through the wall? Or did he fire through the ceiling or floor?"

"As I said before, there is no secret panel in this room," was Britz's rejoinder.

"Then you believe Mr. Whitmore committed suicide?" suddenly fired the coroner.

"No."

"He might have committed suicide, and the clerks, out of regard for their employer, substituted pistols in order to make it appear like murder," joined Greig.

"Perhaps," replied Britz. "Relatives and friends frequently endeavor to give a case of suicide the aspect of murder."

"But you don't really believe it of this case?" asked the coroner.

"I do not," confessed Britz.

"Then your theory must be that some invisible person fired a silent shot"—the coroner paused a moment, then as if struck by a sudden thought—"of course, a Maxim muffler might have deadened the sound of the pistol."

"The office boy would have heard the click of the hammer," interposed Britz.

The coroner repressed with difficulty the smile that struggled to his lips.

"Lieutenant," he said disparagingly, "you don't attribute this crime to the work of spirits, do you?"

"No," laughed Britz. "Spirits don't murder people outside of story books. No ghostly significance attaches to the murder of Mr. Whitmore."

"Well, what is your theory?" demanded the coroner.

"I haven't any—as yet. I shall wait until I'm in possession of more facts before formulating one. Of this I am certain, however. Mr. Whitmore came down here to-day expecting to meet death. In fact, he had prepared himself for it by destroying or secreting all his personal papers. More than that I am not prepared to say at present."

"Is there anything further that I can do?"

"Nothing, coroner, beyond ordering an immediate autopsy."

"Very well," replied the coroner, preparing to go. He was about to step out of the room when his footsteps were halted by an approaching figure that tore down the aisle as if under the stress of great excitement. The figure did not pause at the door but brushed past the official, halting abruptly before the body of the slain man.

"Dead!" he moaned, and the single word conveyed to his hearers the darting agony which rent him. For a long moment the newcomer stood, bowed with unutterable grief, holding the hand of the dead man, as if he would joyfully impart to those lifeless fingers, the largest measure of his own vitality. Reluctantly he relinquished the limp hand, and the effort cost him a pang.

As he turned from the rigid features staring vacantly up at him, he was sobbing inwardly. His handsome face was contorted as if in physical pain, his head drooped as if his shoulders had suddenly grown too weak to bear its weight.

"Who are you, sir?" the coroner's voice broke the stillness.

The wave of sorrow which swept over the man seemed to deprive him of the faculty of speech. He looked about him in a bewildered way, as if unable to comprehend the presence of the others.

He looked about him in a bewildered way

"You knew Mr. Whitmore?" the coroner inquired mildly.

"Yes, I was his confidential secretary," the answer came in weak tones.

The coroner and the two detectives exchanged significant glances.

"Then you are Mr. Beard?" the former inquired.

"Yes."

"Can you throw any light on the murder—have you any idea as to who could have done it?"

As the weighty import of the query slowly dawned on Beard's consciousness, his face contracted until it took on the expression of one whose mental vision is gradually clearing; before whose dazed mind certain images are again taking compact shape, revealing themselves out of the surrounding darkness, sharply cut like figures illumined by the long-stretching rays of a powerful searchlight.

Britz noted the changing expression of the man's face with lynxlike eagerness. There was something touching, pathetic, in the utter desolation which the secretary felt at his employer's death. Then, suddenly, a burning anger seemed to succeed all other emotions, and, in an outburst of tempestuous fury, he exclaimed:

"Collins—George Collins—damn him—damn that scoundrel! He did it—there was no one else! Officers, arrest Collins—you know who he is. He threatened to kill Mr. Whitmore, came down here every day for a month to do it. I'll send that cur to the electric chair—why should I shield him?"

"Precisely," agreed the coroner. "Now, calm yourself and tell us all about Collins."

Beard had been carried away by the storm of resentment that had swept his mind. He had uttered a direct accusation, something which it was farthest from his purpose to do. Caution had been his life-long habit. It had deserted him for the instant, but only for the instant. The next moment it had returned, to abide with him throughout the rest of the examination.

"This Mr. Collins—can you explain how he got in here without being observed by the clerks?" asked the coroner.

"No," snapped the secretary.

"What motive had he for killing Mr. Whitmore?" the coroner fired at him.

"None that I know of," declared Beard.

"Well, tell us in your own way what connection Mr. Collins had with this crime," the coroner said persuasively.

"I have nothing to tell."

It was manifest that the secretary regretted his first outburst against Collins and was now prepared to counter every effort of his questioner. The coroner, however, was not to be easily repulsed.

"This, sir, is a solemn inquest into the death of Herbert Whitmore," he informed the other. "I am now holding court, as authorized by the statute. You will regard yourself as a duly summoned witness. Raise your right hand!"

Beard lifted a trembling hand above his head.

"You do solemnly swear to tell the truth, the whole truth, and nothing but the truth!" intoned the official. Producing pencil and paper he prepared to record the answers of the witness.

"You have accused one George Collins of the crime of murder," he pursued. "Are you prepared to substantiate that accusation with proof?"

"I do not accuse anyone of murder and I have no proof," asserted Beard.

The coroner decided to try a new tack.

"Where did Mr. Whitmore spend the past six weeks?"

"I decline to tell," Beard answered firmly.

"On what ground do you refuse to answer?"

The secretary shifted uneasily from one position to another. His eyes roved about the room, finally studying the ceiling as if trying to discover written thereon some means out of his dilemma.

"I decline to answer—on the ground that my reply might tend to incriminate or degrade me. I'm sorry, but I must invoke my constitutional privilege."

Had a tongue of flame shot from the witness's mouth it could not have produced greater amazement. The coroner and the detectives regarded each other as if uncertain whether they had heard aright. The changed attitude of the witness could only denote that he feared to involve himself. He, who had been so quick to accuse another, now appeared intent only on shielding himself.

"You have found the customary refuge of guilty men," the coroner frowned at the witness. "In the presence of murder, all honest men speak frankly. What motive have you in concealing Mr. Whitmore's whereabouts during his absence from his office?"

"I must decline to say anything further until I have consulted with counsel," the secretary answered readily.

Certainly the two last replies smacked strongly of guilt, or at least, criminal knowledge. If not the actual murderer, he might be an accessory before the fact. So thought the coroner, and the cold gleam of authority in his eyes betrayed his belief.

"Since you won't speak, it is my duty to commit you to jail," he declared.

"On what charge?" demanded the witness.

"On suspicion of being involved in the crime."

The secretary made no effort to combat the coroner's resolve. He simply bowed his head meekly, ready to submit. Britz, however, who had caught every fleeting emotion that passed across the witness's countenance, was not prepared to see Beard silenced through intimidation.

"Coroner," he said, "suppose you adjourn the inquest for the present? I want to take Mr. Beard with me to Mr. Whitmore's home. He may be of service there."

"Very well," reluctantly agreed the coroner. "Take him!"

CHAPTER VI

Had Herbert Whitmore, in a spirit of diabolical fun, resolved to present the New York police with a baffling murder mystery, he could not have carried out the design more effectively than in the manner of his taking off. Not a clue to the perpetrator of the crime or the manner of its accomplishment, was found in the merchant's home. There were not wanting signs of hasty destruction, but the obliteration of all possible leads had been complete.

Two hours were consumed in the search of the house, and all the while Beard looked on silently, offering neither help nor hindrance. Britz, pursuing the search with the help of Greig, put an occasional question to the secretary, but the almost invariable reply was a non-committal shrug of the shoulders.

"Since you won't tell us anything about Mr. Whitmore, kindly inform me where *you* spent the morning?" demanded Britz.

"Up to ten o'clock I was in this house," the secretary replied. "Then I visited the office of the Garfield Safe Deposit Company. I remained in the vaults, assorting Mr. Whitmore's papers until three o'clock. From there I came directly to the iron works."

"In other words, you have a complete alibi with which to meet a charge of murder?"

"Between the time that Mr. Whitmore entered his office and the time he was found dead, I was at the vault, continuously within sight of two guards," declared Beard.

The butler and the other servants were entirely empty of helpful knowledge concerning the crime. All of them united in declaring that Mr. Whitmore had left the house six weeks ago, that no one had seen him leave and he had not been back. Mr. Beard had taken charge of his affairs, in fact he had come to the house to live. None of them had seen Mr. Whitmore since the night of his disappearance, nor had they received any word from him. While they had not accepted unequivocally Mr. Beard's assurance that their employer was on a business trip, nevertheless they had no other knowledge concerning their master's whereabouts and therefore did not openly question Beard's assertions.

"Mr. Beard," said Britz, when he had finished questioning the servants, "I shall not arrest you for the present. But you will hold yourself in readiness to appear at Police Headquarters whenever I may want you."

"I shall not leave the city," promised Beard.

"Very well. Now kindly leave the house," requested Britz.

The secretary left reluctantly, as if unwilling to permit the detectives to be alone with the servants. But he offered no resistance as Britz escorted him to the door and closed it behind him. Relieved of Beard's presence, the detective summoned the butler.

"Who visited Mr. Whitmore on the night he disappeared?" Britz said sharply.

"A lady," answered the butler.

"Who was she?"

"I don't know. I had never seen her before."

"Did you see Mr. Whitmore after her departure?"

"Yes, sir, in the library."

"Did he say anything?"

"He asked me about a letter I had mailed."

"Did you observe the address on the letter?"

"Yes, sir. It was addressed to Mrs. George Collins, at Delmore Park."

"Was the lady whom you admitted that night Mrs. Collins?"

"I don't believe so. I don't know Mrs. Collins, but it couldn't have been she, for Mr. Whitmore did not seem to know the visitor."

"Thank you," said Britz, extending his card. "If Mr. Beard should discharge the servants, please call me up at Police Headquarters."

"Yes, sir," promised the butler.

Britz donned his hat and coat.

"Come on, Greig," he called to his assistant. "We're going to Delmore Park."

Outside, they found the newsboys shrieking the crime. The afternoon papers had worked themselves into typographic frenzy over it. Britz guessed that the coroner had primed the reporters with all the facts which had been ascertained at the office, and the reporters, exercising a lively fancy, had created a mystery that was calculated to absorb newspaper readers for many days. As Britz perused the news sheets on the way to the Grand Central Station, he noted with a smile that the reporters shared with the coroner and the employés of the iron works, the same mystification as to how the assassin managed to reach his victim without revealing himself to the clerks in the office.

"It is inexplicable to me how the murderer got in and out of the private office," one of the newspapers quoted the head clerk. "He must have worn the fabled invisible cloak," was the only explanation he could offer.

"It's uncanny," another clerk was quoted. "I sat at the third desk from Mr. Whitmore's door all morning and I'm ready to swear no one entered or left that office. He could not have committed suicide, for I would have heard the shot. He came down this morning, after an absence of six weeks, pleasant and amiable as usual. We all loved him, all of us at one time or another experienced his kindness. Any intimation that we are shielding the murderer is absurd. Had we seen him, he never would have left the office alive."

Dropping the paper, Britz sought in his pocket for the leather card case in which he had deposited the needle earlier in the afternoon. After scrutinizing it carefully, he replaced it in the case with an air of satisfaction.

"Greig," he said, moving his head slightly to one side, so as to face his assistant, "what do you make of the case?"

"Just this, Lieutenant!" He paused as if in deep reflection. "We've got to decide whether those clerks are telling the truth. If we accept their statement that they saw no one enter Whitmore's office and heard no shot—"

"I have already accepted their statement as the truth," interrupted Britz.

"The possibility of suicide is eliminated, of course," pursued Greig. "The pistol we found is brand new and has never been fired. Certainly Whitmore didn't shoot himself and then swallow the gun. And since the clerks are sure that no one entered or left the office, why, the only explanation I can give is that some supernatural agency was employed to bring about Whitmore's death."

Britz bestowed on his assistant a tolerant smile.

"Then I suppose we might as well charge the crime up to the spirits and drop the case!" he said ironically. "No, Greig, we're not going on a still hunt for murderous, disembodied shades. We're going after living people—and we're not going very far. What puzzles you and the clerks—how anyone managed to get to him and fire the shot—is so simple that I'm surprised you're worrying over it. I have already solved that."

Greig stared at his superior in undisguised amazement.

"Why—er—how was it done?" he stammered.

In reply, Britz produced the needle which he had found at the feet of the murdered man.

"Examine this and see if it doesn't solve the puzzle," he said.

Greig looked a long while at the long, thin, glistening instrument.

"There's blood half-way down from the point," he commented audibly. "But I don't see what it explains."

"Of itself, it wouldn't mean much," admitted Britz. "But taken in connection with the fully loaded pistol and the lack of powder marks about the bullet wound, it explains fully why none of the men in the office saw the murderer."

"But—but how do you figure it out?" asked Greig, more puzzled than ever.

"I shall not reveal that at present," answered Britz. "It will help our investigation to permit the murderer to believe that we don't know how he got to Whitmore. From the statements we have obtained, it is evident that conflicting interests are involved in the crime. We shall direct our energies toward bringing these adverse elements into active conflict, and, in the heat of battle, the murderer will be revealed."

They had reached Grand Central Station, and, luckily, had to wait only ten minutes before boarding a train for Delmore Park. During the short journey Britz fell into one of his deep silences, from which Greig did not disturb him until the train drew into the Delmore Park station.

Lieutenant Britz was too experienced a detective to rush unprepared into the home of the Collinses in the hope of obtaining incriminating evidence. In fact, he had determined not to visit the Collins house, but to devote himself to ascertaining something about the life and habits of the man whose name figured so conspicuously in the present stage of the investigation.

It was seven-thirty when the two detectives entered the home of the village postmaster and revealed their identity. The postmaster, a middle-aged, heavy-set man, appeared tired after his day's work. He was familiar with all the gossip of the wealthy residents of the park, and he quickly found new energy when the opportunity to display his knowledge was offered.

"That man Collins is a no good fellow," he confided glibly. "Just a bum—that's all he is. Stays out all night and sleeps all morning. His wife is a fine woman and I don't see how she stood for him all this time. Six weeks ago everybody around here knew that they had separated. She went to her brother's house—Lester Ward. But last night they seemed to be reconciled again. I saw Ward and Collins and Mrs. Collins at the station together and I heard them say they were going to the opera. That was the first time I'd seen Collins and his wife together since they separated. And this morning the postman told me that Mrs. Collins had spent the night in her own house—that she and her husband evidently had decided to live together again."

The postmaster paused reflectively, as if trying to read the meaning behind this unexpected reunion of the Collinses.

"Did you hear what brought about the break six weeks ago?" asked Britz.

"No, we had a lot of excitement around here just then," said the postmaster, his lips curling into a reminiscent smile. "That was the day of the robbery—or the attempted robbery." Aware that his visitors had begun to display increased interest, he proceeded with more deliberation, as if trying to heighten their curiosity. "The night before the Collinses separated, or about two o'clock that morning I should say, a fellow tried to break into the post office. Luckily there was a meeting of the lodge that night and a sociable after it. On the way home, Hiram Barker and Syd Johnson passed the post office just as the robber was forcing the door. They landed on him and took him to the lock-up. I notified the post office people down in New York and he was taken there for trial."

"Well, what happened?" Britz asked.

"The newspapers didn't seem to take much notice of the case," replied the postmaster regretfully. "A paragraph or two was all they gave it. A week ago the fellow pleaded guilty and was sentenced to two years and six months in the Atlanta prison."

"What was his name?" inquired Britz.

"He gave it as John Travis."

"Rather an unusual name for a post office robber," commented Greig.

"He was a peculiar fellow, all right," declared the postmaster. "Wouldn't say a word to anybody. Just took his medicine without a whimper."

For a half hour the two detectives were entertained with gossip of the wealthy colony but when they left they were in possession of the life histories of Mrs. Collins, Collins and Ward.

Out in the street Britz consulted his watch.

"We've just got time to catch the eight-forty for New York," he said. "I guess we won't visit the Collinses to-night."

"Do you perceive any connection between the murder of Whitmore and the attempted post office robbery?" asked Greig.

"There may be," said Britz. "I'm going to Headquarters now to map out plans. This investigation will have to be pursued systematically in order to obtain results."

Three quarters of an hour later Britz was at his desk in Police Headquarters, studying the various ramifications of the case. Occasionally he scribbled a note and laid it aside for future reference. He was attacking the problem just as a business man might proceed with a commercial proposition—viewing it from all angles and arranging a programme for his subordinates to follow. At least half a dozen channels needed to be explored, all of which offered possibilities in the way of clues. On a typewritten sheet before him were the names of a score of men available for new cases. Britz pondered the list, carefully weighing the qualifications of each man, estimating his capability, his persistency, his resourcefulness. At last he checked off eight names, and, summoning a uniformed doorman, directed that the eight men be ordered to report to him forthwith.

"Officer Muldoon of the Eighth Precinct is waiting to see you," the doorman informed him.

"Show him in," said Britz.

Muldoon entered with the mysterious air of one who has important information to impart and does not intend that his hearer shall underestimate its importance.

"I think I've got a line on this Whitmore case," he began.

"Well, what is it?" Britz asked curtly.

"Just six weeks ago last night I was patroling Fifth avenue in front of the Whitmore house. I saw a lady come out and enter a taxicab. She was a beauty—fine looking and dressed like a queen. In the half-open doorway of the house Mr. Whitmore stood, watching her descend the steps. Both he and she looked as if they'd been quarreling."

"Anything more?" Britz asked impatiently.

"No, sir," the policeman admitted.

"Would you know her again if you saw her?"

"I surely would."

"Very well. Inform your precinct commander that you have been temporarily assigned to Headquarters and remain outside until I send for you."

Muldoon, happy to find himself relieved of patrol duty and assigned to this important case, proceeded toward the door, a broad smile illumining the wide area of his dull face. He shut the door softly behind him, but reopened it almost immediately, a look of bewilderment in his eyes.

"The woman—the one I saw—she's outside talkin' to Detective Greig!" he gasped.

Britz shot one quick glance at him, then said:

"Remain outside until I send for you."

Five minutes later and the door opened again, this time to admit Greig and a woman—a woman so perceptibly under the influence of overpowering emotions as to cause her to stagger rather than walk into the room. As she stood with hands resting on Britz's desk, she suddenly felt herself seized with a desire to weep. Wiping the moisture from the corners of her eyes, she accepted the chair which Greig offered, settling herself in it as if she had come for a long stay.

She felt herself seized with a desire to weep

There was an awkward pause, which was broken by Greig:

"This lady, Miss Strong, has valuable information."

She turned her moistened eyes on Britz, who, through half-closed lids, was endeavoring to appraise her.

Keen student of human nature that he was, quick as he was to gather those little details of personal appearance which, to the trained eye, reveal with pitiless accuracy the innermost character of a human being, Britz was unable to form any satisfactory estimate of her. Outwardly, she had the appearance of a woman crushed beneath a great grief. Yet, there appeared to be something insincere in her sorrow, something calculating in her hesitancy. These contradictions in her manner puzzled and annoyed him, for experience had taught the detective to be wary of women informers. So he waited for her to speak.

"I wish to deliver the murderer of Mr. Whitmore," she said, stifling a sob.

Britz nodded encouragingly, but she appeared in no haste to proceed. Instead, she permitted her gaze to alternate between him and Greig, as if trying to read the effect of her words in their impassive faces.

Her pause might have been that of the consummate actress waiting to note the effect of her artfully delivered line; it might have been the timorous uncertainty of a child affrighted at its own boldness.

"The murderer will be at my home at eleven to-night," she went on in the same seemingly artless way.

"And you are preparing a trap for his capture?" inquired Britz, deliberately conveying to her the incredulity which he felt.

"No, not a trap," she dissented. "I am determined to see justice done."

Britz was too well aware of the average woman's distorted notion of abstract justice to accept her statement at its face value. Woman by her very nature is incapable of appreciating or applying impartial justice, and her incapacity grows in proportion to her immediate interest in the matter involved. This latter might apply with equal force to the average man; but man, less governed by emotions, will permit his sense of justice to prevail when not blinded by personal interest. Abstract justice will frequently appeal to him and he will act with rational regard for its proper application. To a woman's eyes, however, justice invariably shapes itself as her emotions dictate.

Britz, mindful of the fact that with a woman justice and self-interest are inextricably interwoven, immediately began to search for the visitor's selfish motive in offering to surrender the murderer, if, indeed, she meant to surrender the real perpetrator of the crime and not to shield him behind someone against whom she held a grievance.

"Who is the man you wish to surrender?" he asked with aggravating calmness.

"George Collins," she replied without hesitancy.

"What evidence have you that he committed the crime?"

"He often threatened to kill Mr. Whitmore. He told me of his intention innumerable times in the past six weeks."

"Have you any evidence bearing on the act itself—on the killing, I mean?"

"How can I have?" she replied with a faint smile. "He didn't invite me to see him do it."

"Then you simply believe he committed the murder because he had threatened to do so?"

In a carefully planned murder it is always safe to mistrust the obvious. Beard's outburst against Collins had seemed a genuine eruption of uncontrollable emotions, at first. But his subsequent conduct had given his words the aspect of shrewd premeditation. Now she appeared intent on fastening guilt on Collins. Her very anxiety to do so implied a hidden motive. It was necessary to be on guard against trickery.

Evidently she sensed Britz's lack of confidence, for she hastened to say:

"I know why he wanted to kill Mr. Whitmore. It was because Mrs. Collins was preparing to obtain a divorce in order to marry Mr. Whitmore. She had confessed her love for Mr. Whitmore and Collins had intercepted a letter from the merchant in which he urged her to obtain the divorce."

"When did Collins intercept the letter?" quickly asked Britz.

"On the morning Mr. Whitmore disappeared."

Here was something tangible at last. Not direct evidence that Collins was guilty, but circumstantial evidence of the highest importance. Not only had he threatened to kill the merchant, but he had motive for the crime, and a motive which could be established easily in a court of law.

"You say Collins will be at your house at eleven to-night?" inquired Britz.

"Yes," she answered, an eager light in her eyes. "And if you care to be there and will listen, you shall hear him confess the crime."

Her words and the tone of certainty in which she spoke almost dazed Greig. Even Britz had to struggle hard against betraying his amazement.

The whole thing seemed incredible—yet the detectives had experienced more incredible happenings in the course of their long service.

"You say he will confess?" Britz said mechanically.

"More than confess," she answered. "You'll hear him gloat over the crime. He'll display his exultation before me, and I want you to be there to listen."

"But why—why are you betraying him?" faltered the detective.

Her face clouded, while her lips parted slightly in an expression of intense hatred. For an instant she rested her chin on her gloved hand, staring fixedly before her. Then, with a rebellious toss of her head, she declared:

"I am betraying him because he betrayed me."

Here was logic which the police could readily grasp. No inconsistency about a woman betrayed executing vengeance on her betrayer! Nothing obtuse, or puzzling, or improbable about that! It was not the first time that Britz had encountered such a woman. Convince a woman that her lover means to desert her and she will permit his head to rest unsuspectingly against her cheek, his fingers to entwine themselves lovingly in hers, his lips to linger caressingly on her lips, while her desecrated love is setting the trap for his destruction.

Was this woman really about to spring a trap beneath Collins's feet? Was Collins really the murderer or was she trying to fasten guilt on an innocent man? Was she ready to really assist the police, or was she trying to lead them into endless channels of error?

The questions remained unanswered in Britz's mind; must remain unanswered until the woman herself, should, in some way, disclose the impelling motive of her visit to Headquarters.

One thing, however, Britz determined on. He would not permit his watchful nature to be beguiled into slumberous acceptance of conditions as presented through the mouth of this woman.

"It's now quarter past ten," he reminded her. "Permit me to suggest that you go home alone, and that we join you in fifteen or twenty minutes."

"Very well," she replied, rising and drawing up her gloves. "I shall expect you."

As she walked toward the door, Britz lifted himself out of his seat, and, brushing past Greig, whispered:

"Have Muldoon trail her!"

Greig nodded understandingly, escorted her into the corridor and repeated Britz's directions to the waiting officer. Returning to the room, he found Britz leaning back in his chair, absorbed in thought, the lines of his forehead gathered between the eyebrows.

"Well, it looks as if we're going to get the murderer without much effort on our part," said Greig jubilantly.

"Greig, don't jump too hastily at every bait that is held out," replied Britz, emphasizing each word. "All the evidence seems to contradict the theory that Collins is the murderer. He may have betrayed this woman. She may be yearning for revenge. But it does not follow that he killed Whitmore."

"Why, what evidence is there to the contrary?" weakly asked Greig.

"Why, the very murder itself," said Britz, as if stating an incontrovertible conclusion.

"I don't understand," the other admitted helplessly.

"We have two witnesses who stated that Collins openly threatened to kill Whitmore," pursued Britz. "For four weeks, it is asserted, he went about seeking revenge on the man who, he believed, had wrecked his home. It makes no difference whether Whitmore was a home-wrecker or a man of the utmost probity. It was sufficient that Collins thought Whitmore was trying to destroy his home—that he wanted to marry Mrs. Collins. A murderous fury burned in Collins's mind and he was intent on killing the merchant. He didn't plan to kill and get away undetected. Not much! His was to have been a heroic killing, followed by a glorious acquittal in a courtroom crowded with sympathizers who recognized in him a noble defender of the American home. No secret murder satisfies the vengeance of such a man. Had he committed the murder he would have surrendered immediately and tried to justify the act before an applauding public."

"No, it does not look like the crime of a wronged husband," agreed Greig.

"Besides," Britz went on, "we have evidence of a reconciliation between Collins and his wife. It may be simply a pretense, an effort to delude the police. But from what we have gathered about Mrs. Collins, it is unlikely that she would consent to live with a murderer, even though she did not denounce him openly."

"But the reconciliation occurred last night—they went to the opera together," reminded Greig. "The murder was committed this morning."

Britz bent forward in his seat, favoring his assistant with a tolerant smile.

"Only one reason could prompt a woman of Mrs. Collins's caliber to return to a man of Collins's type," he said. "She might hesitate a long while before leaving her husband. But once she took the decisive step, nothing short of a desire to save the life of the man she loved could induce her to return. Don't you see the situation? She must have had knowledge that Whitmore was coming back. And, isn't it more than likely that before she consented to return to her husband she exacted a promise from him not to execute the vengeance which he had threatened?"

"It's certainly an amazing tangle," admitted Greig. "And I had thought that it was all clear as day!"

"No, Greig," smiled Britz, "it isn't very likely that we're going to arrest Collins. But we'll go to the woman's house and watch developments."

The two detectives proceeded uptown in the subway to Ninety-first street, then walked slowly down Broadway, turning west at Ninetieth street.

As they turned the corner they became aware of an excited group of men and women in front of a big, gray-stone house, the name of which corresponded to that given by the visitor at Headquarters.

The crowd was gathered in front of the entrance, talking excitedly, each asking the other what had happened. No one seemed to know precisely what the excitement was about, but that something extraordinary had occurred was plainly evident.

Britz and Greig plunged into the hallway and pushed the elevator button, but the car did not descend. They waited impatiently a minute or two, then proceeded up the stairs.

On the third floor they found most of the tenants of the house massed in front of the closed door of one of the rear apartments.

"We are officers," said Britz, forcing a lane through the crowd. "Who lives in there?"

"A woman named Strong," someone answered.

Britz pressed a finger firmly against a button set in the jamb of the door, and, in response to the insistent clamor of the bell, the door was opened by Muldoon. On seeing Britz he breathed a sigh of relief.

"Come on into the sitting-room," he said, closing the door on the curious crowd that pressed forward.

At the threshold of the sitting-room, their forms framed in the wide, curtained doorway, the two detectives stood, amazement printed on their faces. Greig's heart was throbbing violently and his breath came in short gasps. Britz, as he gazed on the unexpected sight that met his eyes, stood as one stupefied.

On a couch at the side of the room, her pale face a chalky white, her eyes staring rigidly, a thin line of blood dropping from the corner of her mouth, the woman they had come to see was stretched—dead.

And, standing over her like a statue of dumb despair, was the figure of Horace Beard.

CHAPTER VII

Britz recovered gradually from his astonishment. Advancing to the couch he examined the lifeless form of the woman, noting that the shot which killed her had entered the mouth and probably penetrated to the base of the skull. A small pearl-handled revolver gleamed ominously from the floor, about seven or eight feet from the lounge. Britz picked it up, examined it, then deposited it on a convenient table.

As the detective moved about the apartment, his activity seemed to arouse the others from the half-stupefied state into which they had lapsed. Beard, who had remained standing as if petrified by the tragic turn of events, suddenly regained his faculties and gazed apprehensively at the officers.

With studied deliberation Britz disregarded his presence in the room and continued to busy himself with an examination of the contents of a small writing table that stood in an angle of the wall.

Evidently drawing courage from Britz's preoccupation and from the bewildered inactivity of the other officers, Beard bent forward until his hand touched the floor, and, after groping for an instant beneath the head of the couch, again drew himself to an erect posture.

"I'll take that paper!" Britz's voice broke the silence.

A tremor shook Beard's frame, while the blood drained from his face. Then, a rebellious impulse against the detective's calm assertion of authority possessing him, he made a bold effort to destroy the paper he had picked off the floor.

But Britz was prepared to anticipate the move. Leaping forward he seized the other's wrists in an iron grip that caused Beard to groan with pain.

"Greig, take the letter out of this man's hand!" called the detective.

It was not necessary, however, to employ further violence, for the secretary announced his willingness to relinquish the note. Evidently it had been written in a hurry, under stress of excitement, and was as follows:

"*My Dear Julia*:

"Don't permit your anger to tempt you into any rash act. There is no reconciliation. My wife's return is but a sham, designed to avoid a great deal of unpleasantness. Mr. Whitmore's death has not changed matters. Follow Mr. Beard's instructions and I shall carry out faithfully my promise to you.

"Yours in haste, GEORGE."

Britz stowed the letter in his pocket, then summoned Muldoon.

"Now tell what happened," he said.

It required some effort on the part of the policeman to gather his thoughts. The quick succession of events had woven a fog before his brain, leaving him with but a misty perception of what had occurred.

"I—I don't know exactly where to begin," he stammered.

"Did you follow her to the house?" Britz gave him an opening.

"Yes," he replied. "I got a taxicab and trailed her machine. She got out in front of the door and went upstairs. About ten minutes later this gentleman came and must have gone to her apartment. I waited downstairs. Presently the elevator boy rushed into the street yelling 'Murder! Police!' I asked him what happened and he said he heard a shot and a sound like a body falling to the floor. He took me upstairs and I rapped on the door. This man here opened it and let me in. He said the woman had killed herself. As I knew you were coming here, I made sure that she was dead and remained to see that nothing was disturbed."

"This man was in the room when the shot was fired?" asked Britz, as if to make Beard realize the significance of it.

"Yes," responded the policeman.

"Mr. Beard, have you anything to add to the officer's story?" curtly inquired the detective.

Beard faced his inquisitor, trying to meet his steady gaze with equal steadiness. But the consciousness that he was in a serious predicament, that he might be compelled to meet a serious charge, made him waver. He was struggling furiously to maintain his composure, but his inward excitement reacted on his outer frame, rendering him speechless. When, finally, he found his voice, he turned an appealing glance on the detective.

"She did commit suicide," he declared as if protesting his innocence before a hostile judge. "I delivered the letter which you have in your pocket. She read it, then crumpled it in her hand and threw it on the floor.

"'Mr. Beard,' she said, 'I've betrayed George to the police. I have denounced him as the murderer. They have my statement. They'll send George to the electric chair. I told them all I knew.'

"I informed her that her statement to the police was not competent evidence and that unless she repeated her testimony in court, it could not be used against Collins.

"'They'll never make me repeat it!' she exclaimed. Opening a drawer of the writing table she produced a pistol and before I was able to interfere, the weapon exploded and she was dead. My account of the suicide is absolutely true," he declared impressively,—"I swear it is true."

His face now was as solemn as the tone in which he had uttered the last sentence. Beard recognized that he was facing a grave moment in his life, that it was within the power of the man to whom he had spoken, irretrievably to mar his future, to stain him with an accusation which, even though disproved before a jury, he could never hope to live down entirely.

The harrowing fear and uncertainty written in the secretary's face, produced no quiver of compassion in the detective. Britz was measuring the man with cool, calculating eyes, that shone in their sockets like balls of chilled steel. Long ago he had learned to turn an indifferent ear to protestations of innocence. Such pleas drop with equal fervor from the lips of the innocent and the guilty. And the shrewdest judge of human nature is incapable of judging between them.

"I am innocent—before God I swear it!" cries the guilty wretch in a voice calculated to wring tears from the Accusing Spirit itself.

"I am innocent—before God I swear it!" protests the wrongfully accused person despairingly.

The experienced detective, or prosecutor, or judge, places as much faith in the protestation of the one as in the other. He reserves judgment until sufficient evidence shall have been developed to establish which of the accused is telling the truth. For, he knows that while the guilty man's lie may sound entirely plausible, it will collapse like a perforated gas-bag in the end. Likewise, truth coming from the innocent man's lips may be utterly lacking in plausibility. Yet, it will establish itself by reason of its own indestructible qualities.

Regardless of the statement so solemnly delivered by the secretary, Britz believed that the woman had committed suicide. Not because Beard said she had, but because of the convincing nature of the attendant circumstances. It was obvious that between the woman's death and the murder of Herbert Whitmore was an intimate connection, a chain whose links were undoubtedly forged by those involved in the Whitmore crime.

Beard's conduct proclaimed him antagonistic to the police investigation of his employer's death. To place him behind bars would mean the end of his immediate activities. Apparently he was bent on destroying evidence. Nor was it beyond the range of probability that he was the assassin and was busy erecting safeguards for himself.

Yet Britz was reluctant to order his arrest, for he believed implicitly in the theory of giving a guilty man sufficient rope wherewith to hang himself. The activities of a man in jail are necessarily circumscribed. Moreover, his vigilance is never relaxed. Permitted to roam at will, however, he is invariably his own most relentless enemy, working unconsciously to encompass his own destruction.

For some minutes Britz debated with himself as to the most profitable course to pursue with regard to the secretary. Finally an idea flashed across his mind, and he resolved to carry it into effect.

"Muldoon," he said to the policeman, "notify the coroner and hold Mr. Beard as a material witness until he arrives. After that, you will carry out the instructions of the coroner."

Motioning to Greig to follow, Britz left the apartment. Ignoring the questions fired at them by the curious tenants, they made their way to the street, where they found that the crowd about the entrance had greatly increased since their arrival.

"What's happened?" a score of voices shouted.

The detectives waved the questioners aside and hastened to the subway entrance. In the lighted shelter of the booth they paused, silently regarding each other, each waiting for the other to speak.

"Now that our most valuable witness is dead—what next?" finally asked Greig.

"The immediate necessity is to ascertain where Whitmore was during the six weeks of his absence from business," was Britz's unhesitating reply.

"We ought not to have much difficulty sweating the information out of Beard," observed Greig.

"He's not the kind that collapses under third degree methods," opined Britz. "But we'll discover Whitmore's movements—and without much difficulty."

"How?" Greig eyed his superior in mingled admiration and incredulity.

From the inside pocket of his coat Britz produced a photograph.

"I found this in Whitmore's house," he said. "It is a photograph of Whitmore, a recent one. You will observe that the mustache he wears is a heavy one. It is much thicker than the one we saw as we examined his body to-day. Between the time he had this photograph taken and his return to his business, he must have had the mustache shaved off. It is more than probable that he was clean-shaven during his absence, or up to about two weeks ago. Then, in order not to emphasize his altered appearance when he came back, he permitted the mustache to grow again."

"But what does all this mean?" inquired Greig.

"It means that Whitmore was not away on a business trip," answered Britz. "The statement of Beard to visitors at the office was a blind. Business men don't shave off their mustaches when starting on a business trip. No, Whitmore was away on a matter intimately associated with his murder. And, by means of the photograph we shall discover where he was and what he did. We've put in a hard day's work, Greig," added Britz, replacing the photograph in his pocket, "and a good night's rest will do us good. I shall be at my desk promptly at eight to-morrow morning and then we'll proceed with the investigation."

CHAPTER VIII

Although Britz permitted his assistant to find welcome rest after the crowded activities of the day, he did not allow himself the same pleasant relaxation. He felt no craving for sleep. His faculties were too tensely alert for slumber, an inexhaustible spring of energy kept him fresh and active. There were certain channels in this mysterious case which had thus far been entirely neglected. It was necessary to explore them at once, lest they vanish overnight.

Britz proceeded to the Night Court, where he found the Magistrate dispensing justice with the bored impatience of one grown tired of hearing the monotonous repetition of trite excuses.

Accustomed as he had grown to contact with vice and crime, Britz invariably entered this courtroom with a feeling of depression. There is little enough romance attached to crime. In the Night Court, where vice is on continuous parade and crime only an occasional visitor, the spectacle one beholds is repulsive to the last degree.

Passing down the long aisle between the spectators' seats, Britz entered the railed enclosure reserved for those having business with the court. He held a long whispered consultation with the Magistrate, and when he left he was in possession of a search warrant, duly signed and sealed. With the document securely hidden in his pocket, he proceeded uptown again, eventually pausing before a three-story, brown-stone house, two blocks from the Whitmore Iron Works.

An automobile was waiting at the curb. Britz made mental note of the number of the machine, and, in the vestibule of the house transferred the number to the back of an envelope.

It was past midnight, yet the drawing-room was aglow with light. Britz rang the bell, and after a short wait, the door was slowly opened by a servant.

"This is Mr. Beard's home, I believe?" the detective inquired.

"Yes, but Mr. Beard is not at home," answered the servant.

"I shall wait for him," decided Britz, thrusting a broad toe into the narrow crack through which the servant was surveying him.

"It is rather late to call," protested the servant. "Besides, I don't know you."

"I am an officer of the law," announced Britz. "I have come to search the premises."

In his astonishment the servant insensibly relinquished his hold of the door knob and Britz stepped into the hallway, closing the door behind him.

"You can't come in here!" exclaimed the servant, recovering from his surprise. "Get out!"

Britz displayed the search warrant.

"If you attempt to interfere with me I shall place you under arrest," he threatened.

The perturbation of the servant increased. Being a dutiful and watchful employé, his first impulse was to repel this nocturnal invasion of the house. But something in Britz's stern attitude convinced him that the unwelcome visitor would forcibly resent any interference.

"Can't you wait until Mr. Beard comes?" the servant appealed.

"Mr. Beard will not be here to-night," Britz informed him.

The detective's voice had penetrated to the lighted sitting-room, for it was answered with a painful gasp, followed by the swish of skirts. A moment later the heavy curtains which overhung the doorway parted, revealing a woman's form sharply outlined against the background of light. She was dressed in a dark suit and, as she faced the two men in the hallway she lifted a heavy black veil.

Britz noted that her beautiful face was haggard from fatigue and long agitation, but the excitement in her eyes bespoke an energy not to be conquered by physical weariness.

"You say Mr. Beard will not be here to-night?" she spoke, and her voice disclosed the fear that had suddenly gripped her heart.

"No," answered Britz.

"Then it is useless for me to wait." She moved toward the door but the detective interposed.

"I shall detain you only a few minutes," he said; "but having found you here it is necessary that I should ascertain your identity and the reason for this late visit."

A shock passed through her, as though he had offered her an indignity.

"I must go," she declared. "You have no right to detain me or to question me."

"Would you prefer being questioned at Police Headquarters?" he inquired.

The implied threat had an immediate effect on her. She recoiled as from a blow and moved slowly into the sitting-room. The detective followed her, after directing the servant not to leave the house.

"Madam, what is your name?" he demanded brusquely.

It was not Britz's habit to be gruff with women. By nature courteous, considerate of the weaker sex, he nevertheless realized that soft phrases will not prop a witness who, through sheer desperation of will, has been staving off physical collapse. On the contrary, harshness in the inquisitor, by arousing antagonism or fear, will frequently serve to carry the witness through a most desperate ordeal. In this case, however, the woman showed neither fear nor resentment. Evidently she had suffered so much as to have exhausted her capability for further suffering. She submitted to the other's will like a tired child, dropping into a chair and eyeing him with a vacuous expression.

"I am Mrs. George Collins," she answered his question in a weak, listless voice.

Britz's gaze narrowed on her as if questioning her statement. But the very haggardness of her features accentuated her incapacity for deceit. Gradually the detective's eyes cleared with belief and his calloused nature yielded to an impulse of pity.

"I did not expect to find you here, Mrs. Collins," he said more gently. "I can understand your suffering—I do not wish to add a hair's weight to it. But the conclusion is inevitable that your visit at such a late hour has something to do with Mr. Whitmore's death, so I must ask you to explain your presence."

She leaned back in her chair, a look of meek resignation in her face.

"I came to obtain a letter addressed to Mr. Whitmore," she said frankly.

"A letter which you wrote?"

"No."

"By whom was it written?"

"My brother—Mr. Ward."

Britz tried to guess the hidden significance of the note which had impelled this woman to a midnight visit to Beard's house. She must have known, just as Britz had ascertained earlier in the day, that Beard was a bachelor, occupying the private dwelling with a lone servant. Surely she would not have been guilty of so unconventional an act except through desperate necessity.

"That letter—will it throw any light on Mr. Whitmore's death?" asked Britz eagerly.

"Not the slightest," was her disappointing reply. "It has absolutely nothing to do with it."

"Then you won't mind identifying it if I find it in my search of the premises?"

"Not in the least—that is, on one condition," said she.

"And that condition—what is it?"

"Your promise that the letter will not be made public."

It was a condition to which the detective could readily agree. It was no part of his duty to supply the newspapers with the intimate details associated with every crime. He was habitually reticent toward reporters, yet he was not unpopular with them. For, besides recognizing and admiring his unbending honesty, his courage and resourcefulness, they were aware that on the rare occasions when he took them into his confidence, they could rely upon his statements as upon a mathematical certainty. Not in all his career had he ever been known to discuss in print his theories, or deductions, or half-baked conclusion. In that respect he differed radically from most of the detective force. Whenever he had a statement to make, it embodied the solution of the mystery on which he had been working. It meant that the guilty man was safely behind the bars and that the evidence against him was complete.

"Confidential communications obtained by me are never made public except in a courtroom," he informed the woman. "If the letter has no bearing on Mr. Whitmore's death it will be returned to Mr. Beard."

"But I want it—that's what I came for," she pleaded. "Can't you give it to me?"

"Not without Mr. Beard's consent," he replied in a tone of finality. "And then only after I have assured myself of its lack of bearing on the Whitmore case."

She bestowed on him a glance of such keen disappointment as to provoke a doubt of the innocence of the missive. But he did not betray what was in his mind. Instead, he rose to his feet, and, with a polite bow, said:

"I may trust you to wait until I have completed my search. In the meantime, kindly pardon me."

His form vanished through the curtains and she could hear him ascending the steps. To her ears there came a short colloquy between the detective and the servant, but the words were indistinct and she was unable to gather their meaning. Huddled in the chair, she waited while the minutes dragged wearily, until at the end of three-quarters of an hour the detective's welcome footsteps were heard on the stairs.

Britz entered the room carrying a huge pile of papers which he deposited on a chair. From the top of the pile he took a letter, and, advancing toward her, asked:

"Is this the note?"

At sight of the letter her exhaustion vanished and she held out a trembling hand.

"It isn't that I don't trust you," said Britz, withdrawing the missive, "but under the circumstances I prefer to retain possession of it."

It required no formal acknowledgment from her to assure him that he held the right note. Her face, her eyes, her very aspect proclaimed her anxiety concerning it. Retreating to a position directly beneath the cluster of electric lights, Britz read the letter. It was dated the previous day and was as follows:

"*Dear Whitmore*: Mr. Beard has informed me that I may communicate with you through him. For nearly six weeks I have waited anxiously for your return, but I am in such sore straits that I can no longer delay communicating with you.

"I require for use in my business the sum of one million, two hundred thousand dollars. Unless I am able to obtain the money at once, I am ruined. Were I the only one to suffer by the crash I should not mind. But it means the loss of my sister's fortune, as well as that of her husband. Grace, too, could bear the loss. But the thought of plunging Collins into poverty, under the present circumstances, is what impels me to appeal to you.

"To avert this catastrophe my sister joins in the appeal I am making. I hope, in the course of the next six months, to be able to repay the loan. But it is absolutely necessary to obtain the money at once, for my creditors are threatening immediate bankruptcy proceedings. And that means the end.

"Sincerely,
LESTER WARD."

"So your brother is in a bad way financially?" said Britz, more in the way of an audible comment than as a question.

Evidently the subject was too painful for discussion, for she averted her face as if to hide the emotions written thereon.

"Your brother expected Mr. Whitmore to rescue him?" persisted Britz.

"Yes," she acknowledged.

"And Mr. Whitmore's death leaves him in a sad predicament?"

"Ruin is inevitable," she admitted.

"Which makes it clear that it was to Mr. Ward's interest as well as your own to find Mr. Whitmore alive?"

"Precisely," replied she. "His death was a terrible blow to us."

Britz saw the situation clearly. Ward, rendered desperate by the impending ruin, had hoped that Whitmore would come to his rescue. But the latter's death had destroyed all hope of aid from that direction. The letter, far from furnishing incriminating evidence against anyone, clearly established Ward's and Mrs. Collins's interest in keeping Whitmore alive. Nevertheless Britz decided to retain the note on the bare chance that subsequent developments might give it a changed aspect.

Mrs. Collins, divining with the sure instinct of a woman, the obvious conclusion which the detective had drawn from the letter, ventured another attempt to gain possession of it.

"Now that you are convinced that it has no bearing on Mr. Whitmore's death, may I have it?" she asked.

"Why are you so anxious to obtain it?" retorted Britz.

"Because its possession by someone would be an endless source of embarrassment to me," answered she.

She spoke as one engaged in a controversy of minor significance. But it was plain that exhaustion was swiftly overtaking her, that her bruised senses were near the end of their endurance.

"You need fear no uneasiness from the letter while it is in my possession," the detective said reassuringly.

She accepted the statement as a final refusal to surrender the missive, and, consulting the small watch set in her black leather purse, noted with a frightened gasp that it was two o'clock.

"Where is Mr. Beard?" she asked, as if suddenly recalling his absence.

"He is under arrest," answered Britz in even voice.

Despite the soothing quality which he tried to inject into his tone, she started like a frightened deer.

"Arrest!" she echoed. "Then he didn't deliver—the woman, Julia Strong, didn't get the message?"

She shivered, as the chill breath of a new fear stole over her.

"Julia Strong is dead," said Britz, in the same calm, matter-of-fact voice.

But to the woman the words came like a destructive avalanche. She buried her face in her hands, while her frame shook with successive sobs. The last shreds of her outward composure vanished as before the wind, and she surrendered unresistingly to the turbulent emotions struggling within her. Several minutes passed before the inward tumult subsided. Then, lifting herself to her feet, she said with bitter emphasis:

"Four lives wrecked! Two dead!... Mr. Beard and I alive—but what a future! What a dastardly thing to bring all this about!"

Britz, eagerly drinking in her words, watched her in a fever of expectancy. But she checked her outburst before the fatal revelation for which he hoped, received utterance. With a new shock she recalled his presence, and, as if afraid of having incriminated herself, or someone whom she wanted to shield, walked hastily toward the door.

"Please escort me to the automobile," she pleaded.

Britz recognized the futility of trying to obtain further admissions from a woman in her distressful state of mind. The fear that had seized her would prove a padlock on her lips. So he permitted her to lean heavily on his arm while she passed through the door and descended the steps to the street. Then, helping her into the machine, he waited until the car vanished around the corner.

With a self-satisfied smile Britz slowly ascended the steps, intent on obtaining the documents which he had left in the sitting-room.

"With those papers we'll soon wring admissions from somebody," he said to himself. "It's a good night's work—a most profitable night's work."

To his consternation he found that the servant had closed the door. Nor did his insistent pressure of the electric door-bell produce any effect on the butler. Then, for the first time, Britz realized that the lights in the sitting-room had been extinguished.

Consumed with sudden anger he climbed the low iron hand-rail that protected the stoop, and the next instant the broad toe of his boot had shattered the window leading to the front room. Reaching forward, he found it easy to displace sufficient glass to permit him to step safely into the room. Near the curtained doorway he found the electric switch which regulated the light. As the cluster of lamps flashed up, he looked for the documents. They were gone.

His jaw snapped viciously as he leaped out of the room and groped his way to the head of the basement stairs. By the aid of matches he achieved a safe passage down the narrow steps, at the bottom of which he found the button which switched on the basement lights.

In the rear room he found precisely what he had expected. The door opening into the yard was unlatched. Through this door the butler had escaped with the papers.

CHAPTER IX

The development of crime detection in the last decade has followed closely along the line of industrial development. Just as no great commercial establishment can long survive without systematic management, so no great detective force can develop efficiency with chaos on the throne.

Centralization, through closer and ever more close systematization, has not only been the tendency, but the great phenomenon of the modern industrial world. The same condition obtains to-day in the police profession.

A detective force, like the New York Central Office, is managed much the same way as a big commercial enterprise. Under modern conditions every large mercantile establishment must depend for success on the wisdom of its directing genius combined with the intelligent cooperation of its army of subordinates. In similar manner, the head of a big detective bureau directs the efforts of his men to success or failure.

Moreover, the same qualities by which a man attains commercial eminence will win distinction for him as a detective. Intelligence, persistence, reliability, are the foremost essentials. But these qualities, while enabling one to achieve success in subordinate posts, seldom carry one to commercial or professional heights; to the all-commanding peaks of power and glory. The industrial king is monarch by reason of his ability to give efficient direction to the labor of others. The present-day detective king wields his scepter for precisely the same reason.

As great business campaigns are managed and directed from a desk in the office of the president or manager, so the ceaseless war against criminals is directed from the desk of the detective chief. For, be it remembered that the chief function of a detective force is to obtain evidence that will convict.

In ninety per cent. of all crimes which the police are called upon to investigate, the identity of the guilty person is soon established. The baffling problem is to obtain evidence, admissible in a court of law, which will convince a jury of the defendant's guilt. Even though a person's guilt be apparent to all, the difficulties in shattering the protecting wall which the law erects around every accused man or woman, are frequently insuperable. Evidence which convinces the police or the prosecuting attorney of the defendant's culpability is as likely as not to be found incompetent in court and barred from the record. The result is a verdict of acquittal and all the work of the police goes for naught.

Unfortunately for the public at large, the Lecocq type of detective does not exist outside the pages of fiction. But even were there a thousand Lecocqs, reinforced by half a thousand Sherlock Holmeses, employed on the New York detective force, it is doubtful whether their peculiar ability would prove of much practical service. Their deductions, wonderful and convincing though they might be, would never be permitted to reach the ears of a jury.

So in the end, the great detective is the one who, seated at his desk, with the reports of his dozens of subordinates before him, is able to direct their collective efforts toward a single goal—the production of such evidence as is admissible in a court of law.

Since countless writers of detective fiction have provided the public with a most distorted notion of the methods of crime detection, it may not prove unprofitable to devote a moment or two to a peep behind the scenes at the Central Office.

Captain Manning is the titular head of the bureau. He finds on his desk eleven police slips, each bearing in succinct outline the story of a crime which requires the services of Central Office detectives. Ordinarily he will assign two men to each crime and perhaps the same day, or the following one, the detectives will make a verbal or written report. Out of the eleven cases, perhaps ten will prove to be minor robberies of no especial significance, except to the victims. On the face of them, they are the work of professional house-breakers, or pickpockets or hold-up men.

Manning will deliver a list of the stolen articles to his "pawnshop men," who will inquire of all pawnbrokers whether anything on the list has been pledged. Duplicate lists will also be left with all pawnbrokers with the request that they notify the police if anyone offers to pledge any of the stolen articles.

Other detectives will drop casually into places suspected as being "fences," and closely question the proprietors as to what new articles he has purchased recently. Of course, the "fence" gives little or no information, but he thereby lays himself open to prosecution as a receiver of stolen goods should they be found on his premises subsequently.

Next, Manning starts in operation his most potent machinery for the apprehension of minor criminals. He is aware that about ninety per cent. of his detectives have little or no detective ability. They are known as "stool pigeon" men, and it probably would be no exaggeration to say that they comprise ninety-five or ninety-eight per cent. of the entire active detective force. These men, through intimidation, or money, or the granting of protection for minor derelictions, are able to maintain a staff of "stool pigeons," or crooks, who keep them informed of the doings of other crooks. It is through this source that most of the professional criminals are apprehended.

"But where does the detective work come in?" the reader asks.

It is accomplished by the two or three per cent. of real detectives on the force.

For instance: A burglary has been committed. Part of the stolen articles have been traced to a pawnshop. The pawnbroker describes the man who pledged them, but the description might fit any one of a hundred professional crooks. He does not recognize any of the Rogues Gallery portraits as that of the man from whom he received the goods. Pawnbrokers seldom identify crooks, for it is to their interest to plead a bad memory in this respect.

But Detectives Burke and Duvaney ascertain from one of their "stool pigeons" that Michael Ribbs, alias Padlock Mike, is in funds—that he and his "moll," who may be his wife or his mistress, are enjoying the fruits of Mike's labors. And as Mike's specialty is burglary, Chief Manning rightfully decides that he is responsible for one or more of the recent robberies.

From this point the real detective work begins. The chief assigns two of his really capable men, not to solve any one of the numerous burglaries that have been reported, but to ascertain the recent doings of Padlock Mike and to obtain evidence—legal evidence that will stand the test of the courts—with which to send the criminal to jail. And the chances are that in convicting Mike, half a dozen mysterious burglaries will have been solved.

This is the ordinary routine of detective work. Of course, there are innumerable variations, and yet not as many as most people imagine. About eighty-five per cent. of the detective force is constantly employed at this routine business, while fifteen per cent., or even less, is engaged on work that is not in a large measure mechanical.

As for Chief Manning, his genius for directing his subordinates is inconspicuously employed all the time. But occasionally a more exacting demand will be made on it. It may be in a homicide case in which a wife has poisoned her husband.

Of course, in a case of this sort, "stool pigeon" men are useless, for no professional crooks are involved. So Manning assigns six or seven of his best men to the case. They do not roam about promiscuously, treading on one another's toes. To each is given a phase of the case to develop and he reports as frequently as possible to the chief. At the end of four weeks

Manning, surveying the reports of his men, finds himself in possession of the following:

The chemical analysis of the vital organs shows that the victim died of arsenic poisoning. Detectives have discovered the druggist who sold the poison to the wife. Other detectives have turned in competent evidence tending to establish the woman's dislike of her husband. Moreover, she was in love with another man in whose company she was frequently seen. Then it is found that the husband's life was insured and his death not only released her from matrimonial ties which had become irksome, but also netted her a considerable sum in cash.

Sufficient motive for the crime has now been established. The poison of which the husband died has been traced directly to the wife. But a vital element of the case is still missing. It is necessary to prove that the wife had exclusive opportunity to administer the drug.

Manning now concentrates all his energies toward this end. Obviously, all the deductions of Messrs. Lecocq and Sherlock Holmes would be futile. But through shrewd questioning of the servants in the house he ascertains that the husband was taken violently ill after supper and that no guests were present at the meal.

An analysis of the sediment in the husband's coffee cup establishes the presence of arsenic. It must be inferred that the wife's cup contained none of the poison, for she developed no symptoms of poisoning after the meal.

The servants declare that the wife invariably made the after-dinner coffee in a percolator that stood on the sideboard. On the night in question, she had boiled the coffee, but none of the servants had seen her draw it from the percolator or serve it in the cups. But all of them assert that for a year or more it had been the wife's custom to do the serving, so it is a fair inference that the husband did not leave his seat at the table to help himself to coffee, on the occasion of his fatal illness. No one but the wife being in the room with him, and it having been ascertained that she purchased the arsenic, hers was the exclusive opportunity to drop it into the cup—and the evidence against her is complete.

A case of this nature is not established by the deductive methods of a Lecocq, but by the patient labor of a score or a half score of detectives intelligently guided by their chief. The druggist who sold the poison was found after a canvas of perhaps three or four hundred apothecaries. The domestic strife in the victim's home was disclosed to the police by relatives of the husband, whose interests naturally conflicted with those of the wife. Other evidence was furnished reluctantly by the servants, and, through the collective efforts of all the detectives, the woman's crime has been reconstructed in a way calculated to convince the ordinary juror.

It was because Detective-Lieutenant Britz was endowed with a rare combination of talents that enabled him to direct the work of others, even while participating actively in the physical search for evidence, that he ranked as the foremost detective of the Central Office. Had he been merely a shrewd, capable, resourceful investigator, he could never have attained to his present eminence.

Britz occupied a position subordinate to Manning, but his reputation far exceeded that of the latter. And Manning, conscious of the value of his lieutenant, reserved his services for the more baffling mysteries which the Central Office from time to time was called upon to solve.

He was not jealous of Britz's reputation, for he was aware that the lieutenant did not aspire to the head of the bureau, would not have accepted the promotion had it been offered. As a subordinate Britz was relieved of all the routine which occupied so much of the chief's time, so that he could devote all his energies to the single case to which he was assigned.

Moreover, Manning by purely voluntary renunciation, exercised none of the supervision over Britz which his higher rank authorized. So that Britz having been given command of the Whitmore case, was at liberty to proceed with the investigation along his own lines.

On the morning following the escape of the butler with the documents which the detective had gathered in Beard's home, Britz was at his desk in Police Headquarters at eight o'clock. He had not troubled to search for the vanished servant, arguing that the man would be easily traced through his loyalty to Beard.

The first thing Britz did was to call up Dr. Henderson, the Coroner's physician.

"I am sending the police photographer to the autopsy on Whitmore," he said. "Please don't cut the body or probe the wound until he has taken a picture of the bullet hole. It is most important. Also, let me have a copy of your report on the autopsy as soon as possible."

Britz devoted the next hour to instructing his assistants in the work he required of them. To each man was assigned a definite object to achieve and he was sent forth to exercise all his resourcefulness toward a single end. The cleverest "shadows" in the department were set to watch the movements of those involved innocently or guiltily, in the merchant's death. Collins, the detective also favored with a "roper."

"Fanwell," said Britz to the man he assigned to "rope" Collins, "ingratiate yourself with him as quickly as possible. The subject is an easy mark for a convivial companion. You'll probably find him around the restaurants at night. Get an introduction and spend money freely. The gloom of tragedy doesn't cling long to a man like Collins, and even if it does, he'll try to dispel it with drink. Don't push him for information, but lead him on gently. Cunningham and O'Malley will be trailing him while you're roping."

Having set the secret machinery of the law in motion, Britz donned his coat and hat and entered Chief Manning's room.

"Chief," he said, disposing himself in a chair, "I've ordered the men to report to you on the Whitmore case."

The chief made no effort to hide his surprise.

"Not laying down on it, are you?" he asked.

"Not much," laughed Britz. "But I may be out of town a day or two."

"What is the status of the case?" inquired the chief.

"Chaotic," responded Britz. "But there are conflicting interests, and pretty soon I expect to bring them into violent conflict."

Chief Manning's eyes traveled down the front page of the newspaper lying open on his desk.

"I see the Coroner has sent Beard to the Tombs," he said. "There is no doubt in my mind that the woman, Julia Strong, committed suicide. And for the life of me I don't see just how you're going to connect Beard with the murder of his employer."

"I'm not responsible for Beard's arrest," declared Britz. "The Coroner ordered it on his own initiative."

"Shall we keep him in jail?" asked Manning.

"Yes, let him stay there for the present. He's an obstacle to the progress of the investigation, if not the actual murderer."

Again Manning studied the newspaper account of the crime.

"Confound it!" he exploded, crumpling the paper. "I've read every line printed about the case. I've talked with the Coroner and discussed the case with Greig for half an hour this morning. If it meant a seat in heaven for me, I couldn't offer a guess as to how the assassin got to Whitmore. That man came down to his office yesterday morning, greeting his employés with a smile, distributing the most kindly remarks. It can't be that two or three hours later all those men would join in a conspiracy to shield his murderer. And yet, if they didn't see him enter or leave and didn't hear a shot, how the devil did the assassin get in and out?"

Britz smiled indulgently on his chief.

"When I have examined an enlarged photograph of Whitmore's wound and studied the report of the autopsy, I'll answer your question. That part of the mystery gives me no concern. It solves itself. Moreover, the solution is so simple, you'll kick yourself for not having thought of it immediately."

Manning looked annoyed.

"Your confounded habit of never revealing anything until you're absolutely sure you're right is a damned nuisance," he blurted. "But I suppose it's useless to urge you to tell. I've got a headache trying to figure it out, but now I'll leave it to you."

"You may," Britz accepted the responsibility. "What we've got to ascertain is who committed the murder."

"And when we've done that, he'll bring thirty clerks forward to swear that no one entered Whitmore's room," said the chief, a note of sarcasm in his voice. "How are we going to obtain legal evidence, not deductions against him?"

"By first making sure which of the persons intimately connected with the case did NOT commit the murder, and accusing him or her of the crime."

Manning eyed the lieutenant dubiously.

"In other words, you're going to prepare a lamb for slaughter in the hope that the wolf will come forward and confess?" drawled the chief.

"Yes," acknowledged Britz.

"It's an established characteristic of wolves—saving the innocent lamb from slaughter, isn't it?" mocked Manning.

"This wolf may be a domesticated animal—or perhaps not a wolf at all."

"Suppose you find that Beard is the murderer?" the chief shot at the detective.

"Then we'll release him and lock up someone that isn't."

"That's a new way of capturing criminals—ascertaining who didn't commit the crime," frowned Manning. "Suppose you lock up an innocent party and the guilty one doesn't come forward to confess?"

"Then the others who have knowledge of the crime will squeal," answered Britz. "Persons of refinement may shield a murderer through selfish motives. But they don't permit an innocent person, especially if he or she be one of themselves, to perish."

"Well, have your own way," growled Manning, his sullen demeanor only partly concealing the admiration and affection which he entertained for his lieutenant. "What do you wish me to do?"

"Take charge of the case while I'm away."

"Shall I take any decisive steps if the facts warrant?"

"Chief, no one has ever disputed that you know your business," said Britz in frank sincerity. "Our methods may differ, but in the end we usually reach the same goal. So go right ahead as though I were out of the case."

Before leaving Manning's office, Britz sent for Greig and inquired whether it was Officer Muldoon who had taken Beard to the Tombs.

"Yes," replied Greig. "The Coroner turned the commitment papers over to him."

"Did Beard make any statement on the way to jail?"

"Not to Muldoon. But he telephoned to a lawyer named Luckstone."

"Very well. Now come with me."

After leaving Manning's office, Britz and Greig proceeded to the Federal Building. The Criminal Branch of the United States Circuit Court was in session and they made their way to the clerk's desk immediately beneath the judge's platform. Producing a photograph from his pocket, Britz showed it to the clerk.

"Do you recognize it?" he inquired.

The clerk studied the picture a long while.

"The features are somewhat familiar, but I can't place them," he finally said.

"Pass it up to the judge and see whether he recognizes it," requested Britz.

The judge returned the photograph with a negative toss of his head.

"Do you recall Arthur Travis?" asked Britz of the clerk.

A wave of recollection instantly swept across the clerk's mind.

"Sure," he replied. "Pleaded guilty to attempted post office robbery. Was sent away for two years and half. He's in the Federal prison at Atlanta now. And, by George! that picture resembles him slightly. Only Travis was the ordinary, shabby specimen we invariably get here."

"Who defended Travis?" inquired the detective.

"Tom Luckstone was his lawyer. But no defense was offered. The prisoner simply pleaded guilty."

"Thanks!" Britz returned the photograph to his pocket and started for the door. In the corridor Greig laid a detaining hand on Britz's elbow.

"Why—lieutenant—" he gasped,—"that was a photograph of Herbert Whitmore."

"Precisely," said Britz. "And we're going to hop on board the next train for Atlanta."

CHAPTER X

Three days later Britz and Greig returned from Atlanta. It had been a tiresome journey, fifty-five hours of the seventy-two having been spent in a Pullman coach. But the information which they had obtained kept their energies awake. So that when their train drew into the new Pennsylvania station at ten o'clock, they hastened through the illuminated corridors and out into the refreshing night air, with elastic steps and excitement in their eyes.

A telegram sent en route had kept Manning at his desk, awaiting his subordinates. He greeted Britz with unconcealed satisfaction, acknowledging at the same time that he had grown heartily tired of directing the Whitmore investigation.

"It is one awful mess," said he with a comprehensive shrug of his broad shoulders. "And it appears to be getting worse all the time!"

"Let me tell my story first," interrupted Britz. "Mine's an eye-opener!"

The three men disposed themselves in comfortable attitudes about the chief's desk, bit the ends off fresh cigars, and prepared for a long interchange of information.

"Well, I discovered where Whitmore spent the six weeks of his absence from business," began Britz.

"Where?" The chief's face lit with an expression of eagerness.

"In jail," said Britz, and for the life of him he was unable to smother the smile that struggled to his lips. "Right here in the city," he added. "In the Tombs."

"Well, I'll be hung!" In his astonishment, the chief could think of no adequate exclamation beyond the commonplace one which issued from his widely parted lips.

"Yes," pursued Britz, "Greig and I have been treated to a series of surprises—even now I haven't recovered entirely from my bewilderment."

"Well, go ahead and spring them," urged Manning. "They can't be much more astounding than the one I've bumped into."

"In the first place," said Britz, arranging in chronological order in his mind, the incidents which he was about to narrate, "the man that was captured trying to break into the post office at Delmore Park, was Herbert Whitmore. Judging from the statements of Julia Strong and the butler in the

Whitmore house, it is obvious that Whitmore sent a letter to Mrs. Collins, with whom he was in love. Something transpired to make him regret having sent the note and he decided to steal it out of the post office. He was caught before he had succeeded in 'jimmying' the door, so that the letter must have been delivered at the Collins house. I take it, from the threats which Collins made against Whitmore, that he intercepted the note and that a lively scene between him and his wife followed.

"As for Whitmore, he did a most sensible thing. He kept his identity effectually concealed. Before arriving at the post office he had disguised himself in cheap, shabby clothes, so that when he was captured no one thought he was other than an ordinary burglar. At the police station, and subsequently in the Federal court, he gave his name as Arthur Travis. It was such an unusual name for a cheap post office burglar that I determined instantly there was some connection between the attempted robbery and Whitmore's murder.

"Ordinarily, we are both aware, the capture of an unimportant post office robber, would not be allotted more than a paragraph or two in the newspapers. As the banking investigation was occupying pages of space seven weeks ago, Travis's arrest was not even mentioned in most of the papers, while those that took note of it, buried the item on one of the inside pages.

"Whitmore, alias Travis, had the ablest lawyer in the city to advise him. Undoubtedly Tom Luckstone counseled him as to the manner in which he was to conduct himself in jail and in court so as not to arouse newspaper curiosity. Well, ten days before Whitmore returned to his death, he pleaded guilty and was sentenced to two years and a half in jail. And on the day before he returned to his business, a deputy marshal started with him for Atlanta."

"But how did he get away?" interrupted the chief. "There was nothing in the papers about an escape."

"Arthur Travis is in the Atlanta prison," said Britz. "But the prisoner isn't Herbert Whitmore."

The chief's eyes alternated between Britz and Greig, as if trying to read the explanation of the puzzling circumstances, in their faces.

"I don't quite get it," he acknowledged.

"Of course, the prisoner can't be Whitmore. He's dead. There's no doubt of that."

"Not the slightest," acquiesced Britz. "Yet Whitmore and Travis were one and the same person. Now what do you think occurred?"

"A substitution of prisoners," guessed the chief.

"Precisely," said Britz. "I sweated a confession out of the substitute. He's a poor, sorrowful creature, named Timson. Two weeks ago he was down and out, broke, jobless, starving. He was shuffling dejectedly along Broadway when a man tapped him on the shoulder and asked a few minutes' conversation with him. As Timson had nothing to lose but time, he offered no resistance when the stranger led him in the direction of a restaurant.

"'Here's a fifty-dollar bill just to show I mean business,' the host opened the conversation. Timson nearly went into hysterics at sight of the bill. 'Now tell me all about yourself—if you're the right man, I can put you in the way of a lot of money,' said the host. Well, Timson told all about himself and gave the stranger his address. Two days later he was sent for by a man named Beard. He visited Beard at his home, and there the scheme for the substitution of prisoners was unfolded.

"It seems that soon after Whitmore's arrest, Beard made a deal with the deputy marshal whereby the deputy was to receive fifty thousand dollars to permit the substitution to be made on board the train on the way to Atlanta. Of course, the warden of the prison had never seen Travis, hadn't the slightest idea what he looked like. But in order to be on the safe side, the deputy insisted that Beard get someone who resembled Whitmore, alias Travis, in general appearances. For a week Beard searched and finally lit on Timson. Although the resemblance between Timson and Whitmore is not sufficient to have fooled anyone who knew Whitmore, nevertheless a description of the merchant as he appeared in court, might easily pass for a description of the substitute.

"For one hundred thousand dollars Timson agreed to go to jail in place of Whitmore. The money was placed in trust for him, so as to net him an income of five thousand dollars a year for life. Beard found it comparatively easy to induce the man to fall in with the scheme. In the first place, Timson was that unhappiest of all living creatures, the middle-aged failure. So far as he could see, the future loomed dark and forbidding, his old age was to be attended by the most bitter poverty. Not being a drinking man and being cursed with an active imagination, his plight was doubly hard. Under the circumstances, it could make little difference to him whether he spent his remaining years in jail or the poor-house.

"He seized the opportunity which Beard offered. At the most he had two years and six months to serve. By good behavior he could reduce the term to a trifle less than two years. When he got out, his future comfort was assured. Five thousand a year looked colossal to him—in the most hopeful period of his advancing manhood he had never been able to earn above two thousand a year.

"The day before Whitmore started for prison the trust fund was established and the interest began to accumulate for Timson. So that on the day he leaves prison, he'll have ten thousand dollars with which to begin to enjoy life."

"That is, if he is not sent away for ten years for aiding and abetting the escape of Whitmore, alias Travis," interrupted the chief.

"Well, I sort of pity him," replied Britz. "The warden was present, of course, when he made the confession. Timson can get out of jail on a writ of habeas corpus. Of course, he'll be rearrested immediately and tried, with the deputy marshal, for having brought about the escape of the man that was sentenced to prison. However, if Timson can be of service to us in unraveling the Whitmore mystery, we might arrange with the Federal authorities to grant him immunity."

"Do you think we can use him?" inquired the chief.

"Yes, in fact we need him," replied Britz.

"It is certainly a most astounding state of affairs," mused Manning. "I suppose by this time the deputy marshal has cleared out."

"It doesn't concern us whether he has or not," said Britz. "His case is up to the Federal authorities."

"But when and where was the substitution made?" asked the chief.

"On board the train to Atlanta," Britz informed him. "Whitmore was handcuffed to the marshal when they left the Tombs. They occupied a stateroom on one of the through parlor cars. It is unusual for a deputy to engage a stateroom, or to permit his prisoner to engage one, but no law is violated by doing so. All that is required of the deputy is to deliver his prisoner at the jail and obtain a receipt for him.

"The substitute followed the deputy and the prisoner into the compartment, the handcuffs were slipped from Whitmore's wrist to Timson's, and, at Philadelphia, Whitmore left the train. It is now up to us to trace his movements from the time he alighted at Philadelphia until he walked to his death in his office."

A long interval of silence followed, in which the three men tried to appraise the precise value of the substitution of prisoners in its relation to Whitmore's untimely death. Whitmore had escaped prison only to meet a worse fate, and in less than twenty-four hours after his wrist was freed from the cold pressure of the steel bracelet.

"It was Beard who engineered the substitution," observed the chief.

"Yes," replied Britz.

"And to save Whitmore from prison he took a chance of going to jail."

"Evidently he stood ready with the deputy and the substitute to forfeit his liberty for the sake of his employer."

"But was he actuated by loyalty to Whitmore or did he have a sinister design of his own?" questioned Manning.

"That's for us to ascertain."

"And how are we going to do it?"

"By means of the man he hired as a substitute," declared Britz in positive tone.

"But how—how?" demanded Manning.

"That will depend on circumstances. Now I'm ready to hear the developments at this end."

Manning settled back in his chair with the relieved air of one about to discard an irksome burden. From a drawer of his desk he produced half a dozen long envelopes which he tossed to Britz.

"They contain all the reports of the men," said he. "You'd better go through them at your leisure to-night or to-morrow morning. It's useless to discuss the case further until you've familiarized yourself with them."

As they left Headquarters for their homes, the three men realized that despite the many developments of the case, they had, as yet, barely penetrated the surface. Every new discovery had only succeeded in adding further complications to the mystery. The evidence thus far was fragmentary, disconnected, throwing an uncertain light on the crime. The substitution of prisoners tended to involve Beard, yet it gave not the least hint of the motive that actuated the killing of Whitmore. Nor did it reveal how the crime was committed. That it would prove of importance, of vital significance in solving the crime, Britz believed implicitly. But, such are the complexities in all human things, that the possibility of error is never eliminated. And in a criminal investigation a single error may destroy every chance of success, just as a single error on the part of the criminal may destroy all the safeguards which he has so carefully thrown around him.

At the Seventy-second street station of the subway Britz bade his companions good night. Dismissing the Whitmore case and all other police business from his mind, he headed straight for his home, retired at once and fell into a deep sleep.

CHAPTER XI

Fresh as the early morning dew that hung, a gentle, swaying silver mantle above the ceaseless currents of the North River, Britz awoke and for a long time permitted his eyes to feast on the restful picture offered by the now deserted Riverside Drive. Reluctantly he withdrew his gaze from the alluring vista that spread from his window—the graveled walks, the well-kept lawns sloping down to the stream, the wide stretch of shimmering water sending slanting shafts of silver against the rocky base of the opposite Palisades, and, in the dim distance, the softly undulating Jersey hills meeting the sky line in a wavy gray thread indistinctly outlined in the clearing mist.

Britz's salary was inadequate for an entire apartment on the Drive. But he could afford a large square room overlooking the Hudson in the apartment of a small family that understood the ways of their lodger and ministered to his comfort.

A cold shower shook the last vestige of lassitude out of the detective's system, and, after an ample breakfast prepared and served by the single servant of the house, Britz devoted himself to the reports which Manning had delivered to him the previous night.

For three hours he sat absorbed in silent study of the documents, occasionally jotting down a brief note on a pad of paper or inter-lining a paragraph which he regarded as having especial significance.

When he finished reading, he indulged in an additional hour of thoughtful contemplation, arranging in their proper sequence the meager facts which his men had discovered, and trying to draw from each bit of new evidence its true relation to the crime.

Meager, indeed, was the helpful knowledge contained in the voluminous reports of the men. Mrs. Collins had remained secluded in her home most of the time; Collins had forsaken his customary haunts and also clung desperately to the solitude of his Delmore Park mansion. Ward spent his days at his business and his nights at his home. But around Beard things were transpiring, although the detectives spying on him in the Tombs had been unable to acquaint themselves with the precise nature of the moves he was making to accomplish his release from prison.

No trace had been obtained of the butler who vanished with the documents which Britz had gathered in Beard's home. But of the servant's eventual capture Britz had not the slightest doubt. It was a safe guess that he would endeavor soon to communicate with Beard either in person or by letter, and the moment he did so he would reveal himself to the authorities.

Of the utmost importance, however, was the report of the Coroner's physician. The autopsy on Whitmore's body disclosed that the bullet which killed the merchant had entered the abdomen at the right side, traveled upward through the abdominal cavity, escaping the vital organs in its path until it reached the spleen, which it perforated. The bullet did not pass out of the body and was held by the Coroner as a gruesome exhibit, to be used against whomever might be accused of Whitmore's murder.

It was the path which the bullet had traveled that interested Britz. The absence of powder marks, the disappearance of the pistol with which the mortal shot was fired, effectually eliminated the theory of suicide. Yet, a man seated in a chair, and bent on self-destruction, might easily have inflicted the wound described by the Coroner's physician. Before arriving at any definite conclusion, however, as to the position of the assassin when he sent the bullet into Whitmore's body, the detective decided to study the enlarged photograph of the wound which he had ordered the official photographer to make.

He found the picture on his desk at Police Headquarters. Greig had preceded him by two hours to the building in Mulberry street, and was deep in the intricacies of the case when Britz summoned him. He entered the room, followed a moment or two later, by Manning.

"What do you make of it?" asked Britz, holding up the picture.

"Pretty jagged wound," commented Manning.

Britz produced a magnifying glass through which the three men examined the wound more critically.

"There are two perforations of the skin where the bullet entered," Britz pointed out. "Undoubtedly they were made by the needle which I picked off the floor of Whitmore's office."

"Well, what of that?" asked the chief.

"It confirms my belief that I have solved the mystery of how Whitmore was killed."

"I don't see it," snapped the chief. "If you do, why don't you enlighten us?"

"Because I can't be positive until I have more evidence," answered Britz, unmoved by the other's irritation. "However, I believe that before many days we shall have solved the entire case."

The conversation was interrupted at this juncture by the telephone bell. Britz lifted the receiver to his ear, made several replies in monosyllables, then returned the receiver to the hook.

"That was Watson up at Delmore Park," he informed the chief. "Says Josephine Burden is on her way to the Tombs to visit Beard."

"Josephine Burden!" echoed Manning in undisguised surprise. "The cotton king's daughter! Why, she's engaged to Lester Ward."

"She may be a messenger for Mrs. Collins, Ward's sister," suggested Greig.

"Whatever her mission, I'll soon know all about it," asserted Britz. "I'm going to the Tombs."

On the way to the big, gray City Prison, the detective tried vainly to account for Josephine Burden's appearance in the case. That only the most urgent reason would bring her to the Tombs at this critical stage of the case, was self-evident. The newspapers were devoting columns to it. The more enterprising yellow journals, whose investigations were conducted independent of the police, were hinting openly that George Collins ought to exchange places with Beard in prison. Every new figure in the mystery, every new development, was being exploited frantically in the press. Surely Josephine Burden was not braving the danger of unwelcome notoriety merely to deliver a message from Mrs. Collins, or Collins, or Ward. A less conspicuous messenger would have served them equally well. No. Josephine Burden was on her way to the prison for a reason intimately associated with herself, a compelling reason, one that conquered her innate dislike for the newspaper prominence which she was braving.

At the Tombs Britz held a brief conversation with the warden, after which he was conducted to a cell at the end of a tier, behind the barred door of which Beard must receive all his visitors save his lawyer. The detective seated himself on a small, round wooden stool, hidden from view by the heavy iron door of the cell. But every word of what was said by anyone standing in the corridor, would come to Britz's ears through the grating.

Half an hour after Britz was locked in the cell, an automobile drew up at the curb on the Center street side of the prison and a young woman alighted. Her slim figure was concealed beneath a long fur coat, her face shielded by a heavy automobile veil. She approached the guard behind the barred entrance to the jail with the timorous manner of persons making their first visit to such an institution.

"May I see Mr. Horace Beard?" she inquired weakly.

"Sure, if he'll see you," answered the doorman, unlocking and swinging open the broad portal.

She entered with a feeling of dread, as if the atmosphere of the place chilled and repelled her. It is always thus with persons visiting a jail for the first time. There is something sinister in the suggestions conveyed by the long, silent tiers of grated iron doors, something that strikes terror into the stoutest hearts.

A trusty carried her name to Beard and returned at the end of five minutes with the information that the prisoner was willing to see her.

As if further to rasp her refined sensibilities and shock her, she was escorted into a little side room and subjected to a thorough search at the hands of a stout, impassive matron. To Josephine Burden it seemed an unnecessary humiliation and she shrank inwardly from contact with those rough, though nimble hands.

Being unaccustomed to the peculiar etiquette of prisons, she was unable to appreciate how necessary is the precaution of searching all visitors. Even with the exercise of the utmost care, it is impossible to prevent the smuggling of weapons and other contraband to the prisoners.

Nothing to arouse the suspicion of the matron was found on Miss Burden and she was escorted to the tier on which Beard was confined. As she passed up the winding iron stairs and down the long corridors, catching glimpses of human faces peering anxiously through the grating of their cells, she could not help a feeling of pity for the poor wretches confined like wild animals in their iron cages.

To the ordinary curiosity seeker the spectacle is one which leaves a feeling of depression that abides with one like a frightful nightmare prolonged through the hours of wakefulness. What then must be the emotions of those, who, visiting the prison for the first time, behold one who is near and dear to them peering helplessly, with that look of mute appeal that is ever present in the eyes of unfortunate humans deprived of liberty, from behind the interposing bars of a gloomy cell?

The first flash which Josephine Burden obtained of the man she had come to visit, produced a feeling of horror not unmixed with revolt at the relentless cruelty of the steel bars through which she discerned his haggard face. Beard's form, dimly outlined against the steel door at the end of a long corridor, seemed to have gathered to itself the wan light that filtered through a narrow window at the right of the aisle, and taken on a gray, misty aspect, wraith-like and terrifying. She had come upon him abruptly, at the turn of the stairs, and for a moment she stood silent, overcome by a chaos of emotions.

If she expected the door to open she was disappointed, for the trusty simply withdrew half a dozen paces leaving the prisoner and his visitor to face each other and converse through the narrow space between the bars.

"I received your note," Beard broke the embarrassing silence, "and I can't tell you how much it cheered me."

She advanced nearer the door, and extending a gloved hand through the bars, permitted it to repose an instant in the prisoner's grateful palm.

"I had to come," she murmured, "although father went into a fury when I told him."

"And you came to cheer me—to tell me you believe in me?"

Something far deeper than mere gratitude shone in his eyes, and was reflected in the agitated countenance of the girl.

"I came to tell you that I broke my engagement to Lester Ward," she said in quivering voice.

Cautiously Britz peered at the couple through the iron grating of his cell. He noted the tremor which passed down Beard's form and the furtive caress which he bestowed on the visitor's hand. At the same time the girl lifted her veil, disclosing a finely molded face of flawless features, with a skin of exquisite paleness, and flashing brown eyes shaded by long, dark lashes. As she stood with fingers encircling the bars that interposed between her and Beard, her beautiful face took on a purposeful aspect, as of one suddenly possessed of a new and consuming interest in life.

The news which she had brought the prisoner cheered him perceptibly. But he regarded her as if even now he found it difficult to credit her with the courage she must have displayed in discarding the man whom she had promised to wed.

"How did it happen?" inquired Beard in a voice that betrayed his bewildered state of mind.

"You must have known, your instinct must have told you that I accepted him because of father's urging," she said. "Now that you are in trouble I don't fear to tell you that I wanted you all the time. When I read of your arrest I wanted to fly to you, to be near you, to sustain you. This morning I told father of my intention to break the engagement. And, do you know, he assented at once. But he went into a rage when I told him I was coming here, although he seemed perfectly pleased to have me break with Lester."

A person of duller intellect than Britz, from overhearing the conversation between Beard and the girl, would have discerned the romance in the lives of the couple. Had they revealed it in its most intimate detail, they could not have conveyed a better understanding of it than through the words uttered in this murky prison corridor. It was plain to Britz that Beard and Ward had been suitors for the girl's hand; that Ward's suit was successful through the favor which he found in the eyes of the girl's father. But now, when the man with whom she really was in love was in desperate straits, that love could no longer be diverted from its true channel, and, like an irresistible current that sweeps everything before it, it had carried her to the side of her endangered lover.

Materialists may find it difficult to distinguish between love and passion—may deny to their hearts' content the existence of any line of demarcation between them. But the true lover has no doubt on the subject. Love distinguishes itself from passion, through sacrifice. Passion is invariably selfish. Love never is.

Britz, recognizing instinctively the genuineness of the woman's love, passed over its ennobling aspect, to find therein a potent influence for the solution of the crime with which he was engaged. The girl had unconsciously revealed herself to him as a means to an end—that end being the discovery and punishment of the murderer of Herbert Whitmore.

Had Beard been an experienced criminal, he would have known that no walls have more ears, nor more delicately attuned ears, than prison walls. And that knowledge would have inspired a suspicion of the very bars against which he pressed his fevered face. But being without previous jail experience, he said in a voice as distinctly audible to Britz as if he had been talking directly to the detective,—

"Then you don't believe for a single instant the terrible accusation they have lodged against me?"

"No one who knows you can possibly believe it," she answered in a tone of conviction.

"Dearest," he said, adopting a confidential air, "I could leave this prison to-morrow were I so inclined. They haven't the least particle of evidence against me—they cannot have. Were I to force the issue they could not make out a case sufficient to justify my being held for the grand jury. I am staying here because I want to, because it is best that they should direct their efforts toward trying to prove me the murderer."

Britz, in the darkness of his cell, indulged in an amused smile. So this man was endeavoring to draw the fire of the police in order to save the guilty person! Here was a pretty drama of cross-purposes. Had Beard been sufficiently shrewd to see through the purpose of his detention, he would have submitted to his imprisonment with less complacency.

"You mean that you are offering yourself as a target in order to shield the guilty person?" she inquired incredulously.

"Precisely."

"But why?" she demanded.

"Because I conceive it to be Mr. Whitmore's wish."

"Mr. Whitmore!" exclaimed she, obviously puzzled. "You mean he asked you to?"

"No," acknowledged he. "But I know what must have been in his mind when he died. I know what he would have done, had he lived to do it. Dearest, I shouldn't have hesitated to sacrifice my own life for him. I was more like a son to him than a secretary. And had I been with him when he died, I know he would have imposed silence on me."

"Then the men in his office—they know the murderer and he asked them not to tell?" An expression of astonishment overspread her face.

"No," he answered. "They don't know. They've told the truth."

"Horace,"—her voice grew persuasive—"Horace, you mustn't think of yourself alone now. I can't bear to think of you imprisoned in this place. For my sake you must leave it and clear yourself of this accusation."

He shook his head sadly.

"If you knew all the circumstances you'd approve my course."

"But I don't know them—and it's torturing me." For the first time her features showed the anguish she was suffering. He saw and was moved.

"Listen!" His eyes searched the corridor and the adjoining cells. Seeing no one but the indifferent trusty who was too far away to overhear, Beard continued: "Mr. Whitmore loved Mrs. Collins, as you already know. Were scandal to break over her head—if I did not sacrifice myself to prevent it—it would be the vilest ingratitude to an employer whose memory I venerate."

"Then you are protecting Mrs. Collins?" Her frame throbbed with the conflict of agonized emotions. "Mrs. Collins!" she repeated, as if afraid that he had misunderstood.

"Yes," he answered resignedly. "I know I am doing precisely what Mr. Whitmore would have asked, me to do. And now, dear, please don't press me farther. I can't tell you more—not at this time. When all this shall have been forgotten, when Mr. Whitmore's death ceases to occupy the public and the police, then I'll tell you everything."

When two hearts charged with love begin to exchange confidences, it is impossible to foretell what revelations will be forthcoming. And the chances are that had Beard been allowed sufficient time, he would have unburdened himself of the heavy load that was pressing on his heart. But unfortunately for Britz, the hour for exercising the prisoners confined on the tier had arrived, and a deputy warden cut short the interview between Beard and Miss Burden. She was escorted to the street, while Beard joined the other inmates for a half hour of exercise and fresh air in the courtyard.

With Beard's intimation of Mrs. Collins's complicity in the murder reiterating itself in his mind, Britz left the Tombs and proceeded toward the Federal Building. The detective had seen, had interviewed Mrs. Collins. It was impossible to reconcile her artless, engaging personality with an impulse so base as to lead to murder.

Besides, Beard's remarks were open to more than one interpretation. It was entirely possible that he was endeavoring to shield her name from the befouling suspicion of having yielded to Whitmore, a suspicion which the general public would be quick to convert into an unalterable belief, once it learned that she had transferred her love from her husband to the slain merchant. Should the murderer be discovered and brought to trial the dissensions in the Collins household would be paraded unsparingly in the public press. Innocent as the relations between Whitmore and Mrs. Collins were, they would take on a guilty aspect in the eyes of a world that is ever ready to discern its own debasing impulses reflected in the conduct of one who has been regarded hitherto as unstained.

Reviewing all the circumstances of the case, Britz concluded that Beard's statement was not to be accepted as an intimation of Mrs. Collins's guilt. For, had he not accused Collins in even stronger terms in the very presence of his murdered employer?

It was not to be forgotten, too, that a favorite dodge of guilty persons is to adopt the pose of a martyr. And, in lieu of an adequate defense, to create a favorable doubt by insinuating that they are accepting punishment in order to shield a woman. When artfully worked, this deceit may always be relied upon to create undeserved sympathy.

Were there nothing else to absolve Mrs. Collins from the suspicion that she was responsible for Whitmore's death, the absence of motive would have proclaimed her innocence. She loved him. She was ready to discard her husband for him. She and her brother were looking to him to save them from financial ruin. No, she had nothing to gain and everything to lose by the merchant's death.

With this conclusion fixed in his mind, Britz arrived at the office of the United States District Attorney.

"Where is the deputy who took the convict, Arthur Travis, to Atlanta?" he inquired.

Wells, the district attorney, smiled musingly.

"Resigned day before yesterday," he replied. "Said a relative had left him a fortune and he was going on a long trip for his health."

Britz proceeded to enlighten the district attorney as to the real reason for the deputy's departure. He related all the circumstances that led up to the substitution of prisoners, Wells listening with growing amazement. When Britz finished, the district attorney regarded him an instant, incredulity engraved on his face.

"I can't believe it," he said. "And yet, lieutenant, I don't doubt your word an instant."

"You'll be able to ascertain the facts for yourself," pursued Britz. "What I am here for is to ask your help in solving the Whitmore case. Of course, you'll prosecute the deputy if you ever find him. But I want you to arrange things so that I can promise immunity to the substitute. His real name is Timson. I'm going to wire a lawyer in Atlanta to get him out of jail on a writ of habeas corpus. Now, it is more important that we land the murderer of Herbert Whitmore than that you should send Timson to jail for aiding in the escape of a man who was killed within a day after obtaining his freedom. As for Beard who engineered the deal, I doubt whether you can convict him. It will be a case of Timson's word against Beard's and, since it is impossible to obtain corroborating evidence, the judge will have to charge the jury to acquit Beard. But with Timson up here to be used as a club, I think I can force Beard to tell what he knows of the killing of his employer."

"Well, go ahead and obtain your writ of habeas corpus for the substitute. I'll communicate with the Attorney-General in Washington and see whether he'll agree to the immunity proposition," said Wells.

From the Federal Building Britz went to the financial district to look up Ward. A plan of action was forming in his brain, shaping itself as molten lead shapes itself to the mold. If Horace Beard was stained with Whitmore's blood, there was one man who could be made to direct the finger of accusation against him. One man there was in whose heart bitterness and rancor could be aroused against the merchant's secretary.

Beset by financial difficulties, deserted by the girl to whom he was engaged, Lester Ward would be an easy prey to the acute mind and provoking methods of the experienced detective. If jealousy can inspire hatred, then Ward must feel toward his successful rival all the ferocious hatred of a man resenting a great deprivation. And that vengeful passion must not be permitted to expend itself in profitless inward torture. It was a potent force for Britz's dexterous hands to manipulate, a destructive fury that should annihilate Beard—if Beard was the slayer of Herbert Whitmore.

CHAPTER XII

Like one inspired by a great purpose, Britz moved with the human current down Broadway. It pleased him to think that he had converted Miss Burden's confiding love into an instrument of justice; that by its means he would establish ere another hour had sped, the innocence or the guilt of Beard. What her own feelings in the matter might be, did not concern him. He might deplore the necessity of causing an innocent woman to suffer; but if it were necessary for the accomplishment of his end—well, law and order are exacting taskmasters and cannot pause to consider the injured feelings of individuals!

Britz turned into Wall street, possessed by a sense of elation, like a man about to reach out for a long-coveted prize. Through the knowledge gleaned that morning in the Tombs, he would render Lester Ward pliant to his will; would extract from his unsuspecting lips the truth concerning Whitmore's death.

In front of a huge office building the detective halted, permitting his eyes to linger a moment on a brass door-plate that bore the simple device—Ward & Co.

Britz was aware that the firm was one of the oldest in the district, having been established by Ward's grandfather. It did a brokerage and private banking business, and while not one of the largest houses of its kind, it bore an enviable reputation for conservatism and fairness toward its customers.

The front door of the firm's office led into the corridor of the building, its street frontage consisting of a huge plate-glass window, above the half-drawn shade of which, one obtained an indistinct glimpse of wooden partitions and frosted panes. Outwardly the office presented the same conservative appearance as its reputed business management, and even the clerks, most of them gray-haired and bent, worked with slow, labored movement, as if each scratch of the pen, each twist of the wrist, involved a separate thought of its own.

As Britz plunged through the door of the building, however, he became instantly aware of the changed aspect of Ward & Company's office. The corridor was packed with an excited crowd of men and women, fear, anger, resentment written in their faces. Massed before the door of the office, a score of men were reaching over one another's shoulders in an effort to break down the closed portal. On the outskirts of the crowd, an excited citizen was haranguing those about him:

"Prison for him—prison for the rich thieves!" his thin, piping voice rose above the dull murmur of the crowd. "My confidence was betrayed, your confidence was betrayed—the thief! Why, my father's money was entrusted to his grandfather and his father. It was an honorable house until he took hold of it. I thought my money was as safe as with the Bank of England. It's always been a conservative house until he took hold of it. Damn Lester Ward—he's left me without a dollar in the world!"

The crowd murmured approval, encouraging the speaker to continue.

"I tell you this speculating with other people's money must be stopped," he pursued, gesticulating wildly. "What right had he to use my money in his enterprises? We've been deceived. We thought he would follow in the footsteps of his father and his grandfather. But the fever of speculation got into his blood—and we, and our wives and families are the sufferers!"

Those who were not listening to the speaker were pressing desperately against the door, a murderous fury in their eyes.

Cries of "Open the door!" "Break it down!" "I want my money!" echoed down the corridor and floated into the street. As a consequence, the crowd of depositors and investors was augmented by the idle and the curious, who flocked into the lobby from the street and from the floors above.

Those within the office evidently feared that the door could not much longer withstand the pressure from without, for it opened suddenly and a man's form appeared on the threshold.

"It is useless to clamor for admittance," the man shouted, thrusting back the foremost of the crowd. "It is impossible to give out a statement until we have examined the books."

"Where's Ward?" several voices demanded. "Where's Lester Ward?"

At the same time a forward movement of the crowd threatened to sweep the interposing figure off the threshold. Britz, who had elbowed his way to the door, pinned his shield to his lapel, and, facing the excited men and women, exclaimed:

"I am a police officer."

"Then why in hell don't you arrest Lester Ward?" cried someone near the opposite wall.

"If the facts warrant it, he will be arrested," answered Britz. "Your interests will be protected and you are only wasting your time remaining here."

As abruptly as he had faced them, Britz now swung around and entered the office, locking the door behind him.

"What's the trouble?" he inquired.

"I have been appointed receiver by the United States District Court," answered the man who had addressed the crowd from the half-open door. "An involuntary petition in bankruptcy has been filed against Ward & Co. It looks to me like an awful failure."

Britz's eyes traveled about the office in search of Ward. But the head of the firm was not to be seen. Instead, the detective saw a score of clerks, bookkeepers and tellers seated gloomily at their desks, gazing at one another in appalled silence.

The tragedy of the failure was written in their faces. These men, grown old in the employ of this seemingly solid establishment, suddenly found themselves confronted anew with the problem of earning a livelihood. Nearly all of them had passed into that enfeebled state that comes with years of unvarying routine. Each seemed to realize the almost utter hopelessness of obtaining new employment, and several of them were weeping silently.

Even Britz was moved by this pitiful picture of despairing old age. The mute suffering of these men was a hundredfold more distressing than the wild, helpless clamoring of the horde of enraged creditors. A person born and bred to poverty soon grows insensible to deprivation; for when one is accustomed to little, a little less doesn't matter. But these men had occupied comfortable homes all their lives. From their sons and daughters the colleges and universities recruit the majority of their students. In a small way they have learned to enjoy the good things in life. To be cut off suddenly, to learn that the rod on which they have been leaning for so many years is but a broken reed—it is such men who feel most acutely the bitter poverty of old age.

Britz contemplated the scene about him with a feeling of growing depression. Then, suddenly recalling the high hopes which he had based on his expected meeting with Ward, he asked:

"Has Ward been here to-day?"

"No," replied the receiver. "He seems to have abandoned the office. I've been unable to reach him at his home."

"Well, fortunately I've had one of my men trailing him since the day of the Whitmore murder, so it is unlikely he will get away," said Britz. "Have you any idea at all as to the condition of the business?"

"Nothing except what I have gathered from questioning the manager of the office. I didn't learn much from him but his attitude indicated to me that the business is a complete wreck. South American enterprises seem to have swallowed up all the resources."

"Has the failure any criminal aspect?" asked Britz.

"Of course, I can't tell as yet," answered the receiver. "But these cases seldom result in criminal prosecutions. A man like Ward undoubtedly was advised by shrewd lawyers and the chances are that we'll find he's kept just within the law."

Just then the unceasing murmur in the hall swelled into a chorus of profanity in which cries of "What's your hurry?" "You can't get in!" intermingled. Next, a violent pounding on the door announced the presence of someone more determined than the others to gain admittance.

Britz opened the door and a tall, stockily built individual forced an entrance with an authoritative shove of his elbow.

"Where's Mr. Ward?" demanded the visitor. "Has he—" The man paused as, for the first time, he recognized Britz. "Why, lieutenant, I didn't expect to find you here," he said.

"Peck!" exclaimed Britz. "What brought you here?"

"The chief sent me. He just got word from Delmore Park that Ward has skipped."

"What!" An angry frown overspread Britz's features.

"Ward must have known that he was being trailed," pursued the visitor. "This morning, Grady was hidden in the bushes opposite the house waiting for Ward to come out. Two men set on him, bound and gagged him and left him lying on the grass. A passer-by found him half an hour ago and untied him. Grady telephoned immediately that Ward had made a getaway."

"And the chief sent you down here?" asked Britz.

"Yes. We had got word of the failure and the chief thought I'd better come down here to look things over."

Here was a new disappointment for Britz. The one man whom he wished to see above all others, had slipped out of his grasp.

"We've got to act quickly," said Britz, consulting his watch. "You stay right here. I'll go down to Headquarters."

CHAPTER XIII

Fortune had turned her back on Britz on two critical occasions. First, Julia Strong had eliminated herself as a factor in the investigation of the Whitmore murder. Next, Lester Ward had been permitted to disappear at the very moment when he might have been induced to shed light on the crime. Since all crimes must be proved through witnesses, the loss of two of the most important ones was a staggering blow to Britz. It did not diminish his confidence in himself nor in his belief that he would eventually find the murderer. But to prove his case in court—his future efforts would have to be attended by more luck than had been vouchsafed him hitherto, if a successful prosecution were to be achieved.

As though the adverse fates that had pursued him were content with the havoc they had wrought, Britz was greeted by a rare piece of good fortune as he entered Police Headquarters. It came in the person of Muldoon, whom Britz encountered in the corridor.

"Got a prisoner for you!" beamed Muldoon. "The gent you told me to watch for."

"Where is he?" asked the detective.

"Downstairs."

"Where'd you get him?"

"Just where you said I would. You said he'd come around to the Tombs lookin' for the boss, and sure enough he came about half an hour after you left. I remembered having seen him hanging around the place yesterday and the day before, but I wasn't sure of him so I didn't molest him. This morning he comes to the door and asks to see Mr. Beard. Then I knew at once I had the right man. I collared him and had the nippers on him before he knew what struck him. Also, I relieved him of the bundle of papers he had and Greig is lookin' through 'em now."

"Did he say anything when you arrested him?" asked Britz, favoring his subordinate with a smile of approval.

"He cried like a woman," replied Muldoon. "Said he hadn't done anything and wanted to give me ten dollars to let him go. The papers, he kept saying, belonged to his boss and he didn't intend to steal them. Evidently he thinks he's been arrested for stealin' the papers."

Britz found the prisoner in a state of collapse. Opening the door of the butler's cell, he dragged the shivering inmate into the narrow corridor and forced him against the wall. With drooping head and sagging body, the butler regarded Britz as though afraid the detective had come to execute him on the spot.

Nor did the attitude which Britz adopted toward the prisoner tend to relieve his terror.

"So you thought you'd elope with the papers I went to all the trouble to gather?" snarled the detective. "You thought you could fool the police—eh!"

"No, sir! No, sir, I didn't," quavered the prisoner. "I didn't mean to fool you. I didn't know you were a detective. I know you said so, but anybody could say so and show a badge. I took the papers because I thought Mr. Beard might need them. And ever since I've been in hiding for fear I'd be arrested! To-day I made up my mind to deliver them to Mr. Beard. I was afraid to approach that awful looking jail, but finally I did so and a detective immediately arrested me. He was awfully rough," complained the butler. "He hurt my wrists and tore my collar. I gave the papers to him without any struggle—really, sir, if I'd met you I should have given them to you."

Britz thrust the butler back into the cell and closed the door.

"Won't you please let me go?" pleaded the prisoner, clutching frantically at the bar. "I haven't done anything."

Unheedful of the man's appeal, the detective ascended the iron stairs and hastened into his private office. He found Manning and Greig seated at his desk scrutinizing the papers.

"Anything of value in them?" asked Britz.

"Not yet," returned the chief. "But we haven't finished with them."

Britz applied himself to the documents, his eyes racing through them in futile search of something that might shed a welcome illumination on the dark complexities of the case. But the papers contained nothing of worth to the police. Mostly they related to Whitmore's business affairs, which apparently were in a healthy and flourishing condition.

With a shrug of disappointment the detective flung the last of the documents from him.

"Wasted labor!" he observed to the chief. "Might as well return them to Beard."

"Here is one we haven't examined," said Manning, offering a long, white envelope to Britz. "I don't know whether we are justified in opening it."

The back of the envelope had been sealed with wax in three places, and the seals were still undisturbed. Across the front of it was written,—

"Last will and testament of Herbert Whitmore."

Britz regarded the envelope with covetous eyes.

"There is no law which prevents the police from examining a murdered man's will," he remarked. "I suppose the proper thing would be to open it in the presence of the attorney for the deceased. But we are all disinterested witnesses so far as the document is concerned, so we'll proceed to examine it."

With a penknife Britz slit open the long edge of the envelope and, without waiting for authorization from his chief, spread the document before him. It consisted of three sheets of legal cap, to the last page of which Whitmore's signature and the names of two witnesses were affixed.

"Two pages of minor bequests," commented Britz as he finished reading the second sheet of the will.

On the final paragraph of the third sheet, the detective's eyes lingered a long while. Half a dozen times he reread the significant clause, then passed it to the chief. Manning perused it with widening orbs, finally handing the paper to Greig. The latter absorbed the contents at a glance and returned the paper to Britz.

"So Mrs. Collins inherits the residue—practically the entire Whitmore estate!" exclaimed Manning. "What does it mean?"

Greig bounded out of his seat as if released by a spring. He stood a moment as if to fling out a loud cry of exultation, but the serious expression on the faces of the others checked his ardor. A shade of doubt flitted across his face, but vanished instantly and was succeeded by a look which seemed to imply a sudden clearness of vision.

"Yes, by George! it's as plain as daylight!" he burst forth. "She's the one—I suspected her all the time! Now we have it—the motive and the explanation of her silence! Her brother a bankrupt, perhaps a defaulter. A fugitive, too! Her money sunk, her husband's money lost! She knew she was the chief beneficiary of the will—don't you see what Whitmore's death meant to her? We've deluded ourselves into the belief that it was to her interest to keep Whitmore alive. What chumps we were."

Britz's glance was alternating between the excited Greig and the impassive Manning, contrasting the riotous enthusiasm of the one with the quiet deliberation of the other.

"What do you think of it, chief?" he asked.

"I think we ought to put it up to her good and strong," advised Manning. "Threaten to lock her up if she doesn't explain."

"She's a clever one, all right," pursued Greig. "Went to Beard's house to get the letter that her brother had written! They were begging Whitmore for money. Don't you see the game? Whitmore turned them down. So what was there to do except to kill him and get his estate?"

To the impressionable mind of Greig the evidence against Mrs. Collins was conclusive. The grave, complex problem that had baffled his superiors had suddenly simplified itself. A woman needed money; she could obtain it through another's death. What more reasonable than that she should go forth and slay him?

Britz's more penetrating mind, however, did not find the solution so easily. It discovered a multitude of contradictions which eluded the narrower vision of his subordinate. Nevertheless he was compelled to concede that the aspect of the entire case had changed, that Mrs. Collins now loomed as a figure not to be disregarded.

"I understand that policemen were sent to clear the corridor outside of Ward's office?" inquired Britz.

"Yes," responded Manning.

"Well, send a man down there to call off the police. Let him encourage the crowd to remain."

The lines in Manning's forehead gathered in perplexity between his eyebrows.

"What are you going to do?" he asked.

"I'm going to put Mrs. Collins to the test."

The chief and Greig watched Britz in a sort of dumb bewilderment while he lifted the telephone receiver off the hook and called up the Collins house. After five minutes of anxious waiting, a voice at the other end of the wire responded.

"Is Mrs. Collins at home?" asked Britz.

"Who wishes to speak with her?"

"This is Mr. Luckstone's office," said the detective. "Mr. Luckstone—the attorney for Mr. Whitmore."

Evidently a maid had answered the call, for a long silence ensued while the servant carried Britz's message to her mistress. Finally a voice at the other end of the wire said:

"This is Mrs. Collins!"

Britz pressed the receiver tightly to his ear, as if afraid that some word of hers might escape his hearing.

"Mr. Luckstone wishes me to say that Mr. Whitmore's will has been found," said the detective.

If the woman realized the significance of the information, her voice did not betray it.

"Well?" she exclaimed, as if the subject held but a mild interest for her.

"Mr. Whitmore has named you as the chief beneficiary," Britz continued in even tones. "You have inherited practically his entire estate."

The news provoked no cry of elation, no exclamation of surprise, no revealing remark of any kind. Simply a non-committal "Yes!" It might have been the indifferent acceptance of information which she knew must eventually come to her; it might have been the meaningless affirmation of stunned surprise.

Britz decided he had accomplished his purpose, so he hung up the receiver without engaging in further parley.

"Setting one of your famous traps—eh?" beamed Manning.

"Yes—for the guilty one," admitted Britz.

"You have no doubt that she did the trick?" interjected Greig.

"I have no opinion in the matter," Britz informed him curtly. "I may have a most decided one, however, in an hour or so."

"Well, what do you think is going to happen now?" drawled Manning. While he guessed that Britz was setting the stage for a grand climax, he had not the remotest idea of its nature.

"She knows now that she has inherited Whitmore's fortune," said Britz with slow emphasis. "In view of what has happened to-day, there is but one obvious course for her to pursue. She may do it indirectly, through attorneys. She may elect to do it herself. We shall see."

It was an unsatisfying explanation, revealing nothing of the detective's hidden purpose. But Manning was unable to entice a more explicit statement from his subordinate. So he instructed a detective to proceed to Ward's office and direct the policemen on guard there to withdraw to their precinct station.

"I'm burning up with curiosity," acknowledged the chief, "but I suppose I shall have to wait until you're ready to confide what you're about."

"You'll not have to wait very long," Britz promised. "It's a case now of instant success or instant failure."

Gathering the documents which had been recovered from the butler, Britz deposited them on a small table at the other end of the room.

"You may tie them up and send them to Beard," he instructed Greig. "We'll hold the butler for the present. He may be of use."

The detective next obtained a telegraph blank and despatched the following message:

"*Anderson, Chief of Police, Atlanta, Ga.*:

"Please engage lawyer in behalf of one Timson, alias Arthur Travis, now in Atlanta prison. Have writ of habeas corpus sworn out as soon as possible and explain matters to Federal attorney down there. Adhere to line we discussed on my recent visit. Put Timson, when discharged, on board first train and have one of your men accompany him to this city. This department will meet all expenses.

"BRITZ."

The detective waited until his assistant had tied up the bundle of documents; then, lifting the will from his desk and slipping it into his pocket, he said:

"Come on, Greig! We're going down to Ward's office. There's going to be an explosion."

CHAPTER XIV

As the police withdrew from in front of Ward & Co.'s office, the crowd returned. It flowed into the corridor of the office building, a sullen, silent mob, full of repressed anger that required only the slightest spark to transform it into a roaring flame. They massed about the locked door, gazing at the lettered panel as at a corpse.

Out in the street newsboys were crying the failure of the banking house. They did a brisk business. Mourners everywhere are feverishly anxious to read of the deceased, his achievements and his failure and his demise. And these mourners, gathered at the funeral of an institution that held for them so vital an interest, devoured every detail of its expired life.

Inside the office, the clerks worked with their customary deliberation, tallying the accounts for the receiver. No tentative statement of assets and liability had been announced by the court's representative. He could have prepared a fairly accurate statement and posted it on the door. But he was a charitable man and wished to spare the depositors further anguish. Give them time to recover from the first great shock before inflicting a greater one, he argued. So he postponed the evil moment when he must reveal the wretched condition of the institution.

Each time the door opened and a messenger left, the crowd set on him beseeching information of the financial condition of the private bank. But the messengers had nothing to reveal.

As invariably happens with crowds, the dullness and depression wears off after a while, exhausts itself, so to speak, and is succeeded gradually by a blind resentment directed against the first object which offers itself as a handy target. A sort of mob intoxication sets in, as unreasoning as it frequently is destructive.

And so the crowd now began to hurl maledictions on the innocent head of the receiver. As if he had brought on the catastrophe!

"Why don't he tell us where we stand?" demanded one obstreperous creditor. "Smash in the door! Let's find out what's become of our money!"

"He's in cohoots with thieves!" exclaimed another. "They're all a lot of crooks! What one has left behind the other'll take."

Britz and Greig, mingling with the crowd, neither encouraged nor discouraged the destructive fury which they saw gathering. They knew the psychology of mobs. It is brave with collective courage, but timorous, hesitant, individually. In the absence of a leader its anger would pass like a storm overhead. If a leader should appear, it would be time to interfere; and then it would be necessary to do so before the crowd got into action.

A half hour passed with nothing more exciting than the frantic appeals of the janitor of the building for police protection. Failing to obtain it he implored the depositors to leave. He might as well have appealed to the ocean tide to change its course.

Britz consulted his watch.

"I wonder whether I've miscalculated this time?" he remarked.

Greig, having but a vague idea of Britz's plan, vouchsafed no reply. He remained close to the other's elbow.

Another ten minutes passed and Britz began to look uneasily at the door. A shade of disappointment crossed his face, and did not go unobserved by his assistant.

The crowd was growing unwieldy. It began to exert a slow, steady pressure against the door of Ward's office. The mob was composed entirely of creditors, for the merely curious had grown tired and departed hours ago. Those who remained were beyond discouragement; they hung on with the persistency of despair.

"Oh, let's tear down the blamed door!" shouted someone in a voice more determined than had been heard thus far. "I'm not going home to-day until I learn just what's happened to my money."

"Yes, break it down!" echoed a dozen voices.

But suddenly the attention of the mob was diverted from the door. A woman had torn into the corridor and was struggling frantically to make a lane for herself. There was something compelling about her, something in her pale, distraught face that commanded the respectful surrender of the crowd. They made a passage for her, through which she passed hurriedly.

"Mrs. Collins—Ward's sister!" said Britz aloud.

The words penetrated the serried ranks of creditors like an electric spark. Instantly their attitude changed. Closing in on her, they forced her against the door of the office as though she were a lay figure. All their better instincts, all their upbringing was forgotten in the inarticulate fury aroused by her presence.

She stood, palpitant, a dull stare in her eyes, her frame throbbing violently.

"Where's your brother?" someone broke the silence. "Where is he? Where's our money? You were interested in the bank! You were one of the owners. What did you do with our money?"

At first she seemed not to have heard. Then, a wave of understanding swept over her, and she lifted her hand for silence.

"I have the money," she cried. "You shall all be paid in full."

The crowd moved back, abashed. A silence, the hush of tense anticipation, fell on them.

"Every dollar will be repaid," she assured them. "I promise it."

Her voice, though softly modulated, had a penetrating quality which carried it to the hearing of those in the office. Someone opened the door and she entered. The crowd, evidently scenting some new deceit swarmed in after her.

"What assurance have we that we're going to get the money?" one of them demanded.

Even to her agitated mind it became evident that an antagonistic spirit animated the crowd. After their first surprise, they refused to extend unqualified credence to her words.

"You have my word," she said impressively. Then, as her eyes met the derisive smiles with which her promise was received, she discarded the discretion which otherwise she might have maintained. "I have inherited the money with which I shall pay you," she informed them. "I am the chief beneficiary under Mr. Whitmore's will. The fortune which comes to me shall go toward repaying you."

Her earnestness, the obvious honesty of her purpose, began to exert a favorable influence on the listeners. Despair had deadened the consideration to which she was entitled as a woman; hope now galvanized it into life. The crowd began to draw back sheepishly, as if ashamed of its inconsiderate conduct. Taking advantage of the favorable turn, Britz and Greig stepped forward.

"If you believe this lady, please leave the office and permit her to see the receiver," Britz appealed to the crowd's chivalry.

They filed out of the office, slowly, reluctantly, as if not quite believing what they had heard, yet not daring to display their doubt openly. She might change her mind if they remained; so, out of prudence, they withdrew.

When the last of them had disappeared through the door, Britz turned the key in the lock and advanced toward the woman. She had dropped into a chair which the receiver had thoughtfully provided. At her side, regarding her with an expression of puzzled interest, stood a medium-sized, stooped man, with iron-gray hair and beard, whose cold, steely eyes looked down on her as if toying to read her inmost thoughts.

"Why, Mrs. Collins, what does it mean?" he inquired.

She met his gaze steadily, with a faint smile.

"It was very kind of you, Mr. Luckstone, to telephone," she murmured gratefully.

"Telephone!" he ejaculated. "I don't understand."

"Didn't you have one of your men 'phone me? He told me of the will—that I had inherited Mr. Whitmore's estate."

Luckstone turned his searching eyes on her.

"Mr. Whitmore's will was drawn by one of his other attorneys," he said. "I never saw it. It was entrusted to Mr. Beard's keeping. It vanished on the night of his arrest and has not been found."

A shiver ran down the woman's form. The blood seemed to drain from her face; a new terror gripped her heart.

"I have been fooled," she moaned, "Everything is lost. Money, honor,—everything! I cannot keep my promise to these men."

"Perhaps you simply mistook the source of the message," ventured the lawyer cautiously.

Moved by the woman's distress, Britz came forward, the missing will in his hand.

"Mrs. Collins is right as to the inheritance," he said. "I have the will. You may read it." He passed the document to the lawyer, who read it with undisguised satisfaction.

"Yes, Mr. Whitmore has left you the residue of his estate," he affirmed, addressing the woman. "There will be more than sufficient to meet all the obligations of the banking house. Having some knowledge of Mr. Whitmore's holdings, I feel confident in saying the estate will amount to upward of ten million dollars."

The news did not revive Mrs. Collins's spirits. For days now, every new expectation had been succeeded by a new disappointment. This woman, who through all the years of her harrowing married life, had never faltered in her conduct; who had never wavered in the high standard of her womanhood; whose actions had ever been inspired by the noblest ideals of her sex;—this woman had been selected by fate as the victim of its unrelenting wrath.

The rapid succession of misfortunes which had been visited on her had made her wary of anything that savored of a more favorable providence. So she received the confirmation of her inheritance with a self-pitying stare, as if it must, of necessity, hide some new form of anguish.

"Don't you realize what it means?" Luckstone tried to encourage her. "It means that the bank is saved. All the depositors will be paid. You are wealthy again—far wealthier than ever before." Checking himself suddenly, the lawyer turned toward Britz. "I wonder who telephoned to Mrs. Collins?" he asked.

"I took the liberty of using your name," said Britz.

The lawyer tried to freeze him with a glance.

"And who are you, sir?" he asked icily.

"I am a detective attached to the Central Office."

"Where did you get this will?"

"I don't care to go into that matter now," snapped Britz.

"Perhaps you will inform me why you presumed to use my name in telephoning to Mrs. Collins?" persisted the lawyer.

"Because I wanted to see just what she would do."

"I hope your curiosity is satisfied."

"Quite satisfied."

"Then there is no reason for your remaining," said Luckstone. "I am the attorney for the receiver, and I am sure he does not require your presence."

Britz was on the point of making a sharp retort, but checked himself. He recalled the stern purpose of his visit, a purpose which he would execute relentlessly, yet not without feelings of the utmost pity. For the iron was hot, it was time to strike.

"I shall go," remarked the detective, "but I shall have to ask this lady to accompany me to Police Headquarters."

It required some effort of will to say it. The suffering which she endured had aroused in him a compassion to which he would have found it easy to yield. But having repelled the charitable impulse that threatened to wreck his carefully devised plan, he said with added firmness:

"I am ready to start as soon as she is."

"Why, what do you mean?" bellowed the lawyer. "This is an outrage! What the devil do you mean?"

"I mean that Mrs. Collins is under arrest," explained the detective.

CHAPTER XV

On hearing the ominous word, arrest, Mrs. Collins trembled and grew cold. She looked entreatingly from the detective to the lawyer, as if seeking some explanation of this new and entirely unexpected blow. Britz, noting the helpless bewilderment of the woman, experienced a painful contraction of heart, as if it were ordained that he must share the suffering which he had inflicted on her. Presently she lifted her face to his in a look of silent protest, and he felt a stinging sense of shame at the shabby part he was compelled to play. But he remained firm.

"I am sorry, but I must insist that this lady come with me," he said with a note of sad determination in his voice.

"Oh, you're sorry!" echoed Luckstone ironically. "You'll be sorrier before you're through with this case. This is an outrage! On what charge do you arrest this lady?"

"On the charge that she has guilty knowledge of the murder of Herbert Whitmore," returned Britz.

"It's absurd," railed Luckstone. "Ridiculous! Why don't you accuse her of having killed Mr. Whitmore?"

"Perhaps I may," said Britz challengingly.

"It would be just like you blundering policemen," sneered the lawyer. "Mrs. Collins, a lady of refinement, a gentlewoman in every sense of the word—is she to be dragged to Police Headquarters like a common felon? You have observed her conduct here to-day. You've seen her anxiety for the depositors of this institution. Her only thought was to save them from financial loss. Why, search her entire life and see whether you can discover a single base act that she has committed."

"My interest is confined to the Whitmore case," said Britz.

All this while Mrs. Collins sat outwardly resigned but inwardly rebellious against the injustice which was about to impose on her the humiliation of imprisonment. Now she arose with a sudden accession of new strength.

"Do you really believe me capable of committing murder?" she inquired resentfully.

It was as if she had just awakened from a long torpor and had determined to meet the danger which confronted her with all the weapons at her command. This recovery was precisely what Britz had been waiting for. It foreshadowed fight and the ensuing conflict promised certain revelations which were necessary for a clearer understanding of the circumstances surrounding Whitmore's death.

"Every human being, given sufficient cause, is capable of murder," the detective baited her. "We are all potential murderers."

She recoiled as from a blow. The detective's words could be interpreted only as an intimation of her guilt.

"I loved Mr. Whitmore," she said, deeply moved. "You don't understand."

"Then why don't you enlighten me?" he flashed.

She stood mute, her face drawn in an expression of pain.

"What enlightenment can I offer?" she asked weakly.

Britz's eyes narrowed on her, fixed themselves on her troubled countenance in a cold, scrutinizing stare.

"Who killed Herbert Whitmore?" he shot at her.

The question had the effect of a pistol report. She trembled, her color changed from pale to crimson, she pressed her hand to her heart as if to moderate its pulsations. Before she recovered from the violence of the emotions suddenly aroused in her, Luckstone had come to her assistance.

"Why do you ask that?" he demanded. "A moment ago you practically accused this lady of murder. Are you seeking incriminating admissions? Or are you simply on a fishing expedition?"

"I am trying to ascertain the truth," said Britz.

Luckstone turned toward the woman.

"As your attorney I instruct you not to answer this man's questions."

"And as one who has no other desire than to serve the ends of justice, I urge you to disregard your lawyer's advice," Britz appealed to her.

Between these conflicting forces she stood helpless, aware only of the danger which hung over her. Her lips moved as if to speak, but no word came from them.

"Madam," pursued Britz with increasing earnestness, "the man you loved has been murdered. There is a conspiracy on foot to shield the murderer. Those who know, who ought to be the first to come forward as the accusers, are maintaining a guilty silence. In the eyes of the law they are accessories after the fact. You are one of them. Whether you are the assassin or not, you know better than anyone else.

"All the circumstances point to you as being involved in Mr. Whitmore's death. You are the one who benefits most by his murder. No honest person hesitates to explain away incriminating circumstances. Silence is the common refuge of the guilty. If you are innocent you have only to speak, to declare the truth, and you shall be subjected to no embarrassments at the hands of the law. I promise it."

She was shaken by this impassioned outburst of the detective, but before her wavering mind could come to any definite resolve, Luckstone again interposed.

"Don't let him fool you," he cautioned. "He's trying to entrap you. These detectives have only one object—to convict somebody. The glory of conviction is all they're after. They have no regard for the requirements of truth and justice. He's determined to arrest you and nothing you can say will alter that determination. So keep silent and reserve your defense for the court, where you are assured of an impartial hearing. I'll protect your interests."

His words threw the turning weight into the scale of argument and she indicated her subjection to the lawyer's will.

"Very well," snapped Britz. "Greig, go and fetch a cab. We'll proceed to Headquarters."

As the woman had acknowledged Luckstone as her attorney, Britz could not deny him the right to accompany her to the Central Office. All the way to the Mulberry street building the lawyer encouraged her silence, imposed it on her as the one safe course to pursue.

"No matter what they say or do, no matter what methods they apply, don't unseal your lips," was his parting advice.

She offered no protest when arraigned before the desk lieutenant, and, with impassive countenance, heard the charge of being an accessory to the murder of Herbert Whitmore. But, as a matron led her toward the cells, she began to weep softly and successive tremors shook her frame.

Word of Mrs. Collins's arrest spread through the big police building and in few minutes Britz was besieged by importuning reporters. He waved them aside and entered his private office where he was joined by Manning and Greig.

"Well, Britz, you've certainly given the newspapers a sensation," observed the chief. "But it's going to be damned hard to convict a woman!"

"I've taken a desperate step," rejoined Britz.

"Why—what do you mean?"

"Chief, I outlined my plan to you before leaving for Atlanta," the detective reminded him. "Let me explain that this crime was not committed by an outsider. It was the work of one of a small group of persons. I told you that I would find the man or woman in the group who did NOT commit the murder and that I would arrest him or her."

"Then you believe she is innocent?" interjected Greig.

"I'm sure of it."

"But man alive, look what you've done!" cried Manning. "Think of the torture to which you're putting her! Why, it's unheard of! It's inhuman."

"No, it was the most merciful thing I could have done," answered Britz.

"From your point of view—perhaps!" The chief frowned. "But it's the most distorted view of mercy I ever heard of. I'm an old-timer at the police business, but I wouldn't have had the courage or the heart to do it."

"Don't imagine that I didn't feel badly," said Britz. "She may not be aware of it now, but it was the kindliest thing I could have done. Why, to-morrow morning the papers will be full of the latest phase of the case. Everybody will know that she is Whitmore's residuary legatee. This woman, entirely unrelated to him, whose husband had threatened to kill Whitmore, inherits the merchant's fortune. Her brother's business has been wrecked; wrecked so completely that he abandoned it—hadn't the courage to face his creditors. She and Ward were in desperate need of funds. She obtained them through Whitmore's death. On the day before he was killed she returned to the husband whom she had discarded for the merchant. What inference do you think the public is going to draw? Why, that she was Whitmore's mistress and that she and her worthless husband were in a conspiracy to obtain the money.

"And now what's going to happen?" the detective continued. "Why, public sympathy will be extended to her in full measure. Permit suspicion to fall on a woman without arresting her, and the public is ready to believe every scandal concerning her which the putrid imagination of every bar-room hanger-on can invent. Once you arrest her, the public in its eagerness to damn the police will repudiate every bit of unfavorable evidence we may offer against her. Well, we can stand public reprobation; she can't."

The chief looked unconvinced.

"That's all right as far as it goes," he said. "But you appear to have forgotten Ward. Remember, he is a fugitive. He had the same motive as his sister for killing Whitmore. He also profits by Whitmore's death."

"The only way he profits is through his sister," returned Britz. "And, to assign a motive to him for killing Whitmore, we must assume that he knew of the will. Had he known of the inheritance, do you think he would have skipped? No, he'd have hung on until the will was found and offered for probate! Moreover, he would have informed his most pressing creditors of his sister's inheritance and of her willingness to rescue the banking house. The creditors would never have begun expensive bankruptcy proceedings."

"But if he didn't know of the inheritance, is it likely that his sister knew?" interjected the chief.

"She didn't know," said Britz in positive tone. "However, we'll soon make sure whether she did or not. I shall call up the lawyer who drew the will."

Britz found the lawyer's telephone number and soon was connected with his office.

"I wish to speak with Mr. Sands," he said. "This is Police Headquarters."

The attorney came to the wire.

"This is Lieutenant Britz," said the detective. "I believe you were one of the attorneys for Mr. Whitmore."

"I did a very small part of his legal work," came the reply.

"You drew his will, didn't you?"

"Yes."

"Where was the will signed?"

"In my office."

"Who, beside you and Mr. Whitmore knew the provisions of the will?"

"No one that I am aware of. Mr. Whitmore was especially anxious that the utmost secrecy should be observed with regard to it. The witnesses to the document are clerks in my office, and they were not permitted to read the will. After it was executed it was sealed in a heavy envelope and carried away by Mr. Whitmore. I believe he intrusted it to his confidential secretary."

"Thank you!" said Britz, returning the receiver to the hook. "The seals were intact when we opened the envelope," he recalled to the chief. "I don't believe the contents of that document were communicated to anyone before we read the will. That eliminates the theory that Ward, or Collins, or Mrs. Collins killed Whitmore in order to obtain the inheritance."

"And except to get the fortune, what possible motive could Mrs. Collins or Ward have for seeking Whitmore's death?" asked the chief.

"I don't know." Britz shrugged. "As the case stands, Collins appears to be the only one with sufficient motive for the crime. Yet I am fully convinced that Collins didn't do it."

CHAPTER XVI

At a window of the Cosmos Club, overlooking Fifth avenue, two men were seated. It was dusk, and thick shadows filled the unlighted clubroom, concealing the faces of the men from the countless eyes of the men and women passing in parade beneath the window.

From where they sat the two men could observe the endless procession in the street, while keeping an eye on the door leading from the room into the main corridor of the big clubhouse. One of the men—the younger of the two—appeared uneasy over something, even rebellious at times. His sallow complexion had taken on a muddy hue in the semi-darkness of the room, giving his face the appearance of a compact shadow outlined against the heavy brown leather chair in which he sat. From beneath a slightly receding forehead two lusterless eyes peered apprehensively about the room, and each time the door opened the man started violently in his seat.

The occupant of the second chair was a middle-aged man of somewhat ruddy complexion, smooth-shaven, with an expression habitually alert, yet concealed by a free-and-easy manner and an ingratiating smile that seemed to stamp him as one of those genial souls in whom no harm can reside. Yet the younger man appeared to regard him with sullen fear.

"It's a sort of dirty, underhand thing to do, Fanwell," he was protesting to his companion. "Not a bit clubby."

Fanwell remained entirely unabashed beneath this surly reproof.

"Look here, Cooper!" He moved his chair a trifle closer. "You don't have to do it—I can't make you. But you know the consequences. You know as well as I that the chief isn't doing favors for nothing. He let you stay out of jail because he figured on using you some day. Your day of usefulness has arrived. If I could rope Collins without you I'd do it. But I can't play a waiting game. You've got to introduce me and stand by until I tip you off to go!"

Cooper squirmed in his seat. He might revolt at the other's assumption of authority over him, but he was aware that in the end he would surrender. He was not in a position to incur the displeasure of the police.

Thomas Taylor Cooper was one of those men-about-town, without visible means of support, who always manage to maintain an outward show of wealth. No club is so exclusive that it does not contain one or more members of the Cooper type. Their pedigrees are without blemish. Their social position is secure through a long line of honorable ancestors. But their means of livelihood are precarious. Friends and fellow club members may wonder where they obtain the money for their dues, but somehow their curiosity seldom inspires them to investigate.

The Coopers of society and club life have many invisible means of support. There are the climbers, who are easy prey. Then the tailors and haberdashers are glad to furnish free wearing apparel in return for the custom which these men are able to recommend. Caterers, decorators, florists do not balk at paying commissions on contracts. The society papers pay liberally for society scandal. And occasionally, as in every other station of life, there is to be found in the upper circles of society, an idle and discontented woman with more money than prudence.

Cooper had attached himself to one of these women; and, as their relations grew more intimate, he succeeded in attaching himself to some of her rings. Subsequently he met more promising prey and began to neglect the woman whose confidence he had betrayed. At first her jealous rage expended itself in futile appeals to his manhood, his honor, his sense of obligation. Then it occupied itself with plans for revenge. She demanded the return of the jewelry which he had borrowed on one pretense or another. But it had passed long ago to the pawnshops and could not be reclaimed. Seeing an opportunity to humiliate and punish the man, she discarded discretion, and appealed to the police.

As invariably happens in such cases, the woman came to her senses eventually. Cooper found the climate elsewhere more inviting and remained away until the woman realized that she was plunging into a colossal scandal and withdrew her complaint.

But Cooper had placed himself in the power of the police, and now Fanwell did not hesitate to exert that power over him.

"Collins didn't leave the house until to-day," the detective explained. "But he broke loose this afternoon when he learned that his brother-in-law's bank had busted and that all his money is tied up in the failure. He was drunk when he left the house and the chances are he'll be more intoxicated when he drops in here."

"But if it ever gets out that I acted as police agent I'd be shunned by everybody I know," growled Cooper.

"It will never get out," the other promised. "You needn't have a bit of fear."

The shadows in the room lengthened until it was difficult to distinguish the various objects scattered about the place. The few members that had dropped into the club faded into dark images barely discernible in their broad leather chairs. Then, of a sudden, the lights were switched on. The sharp rays that spread from the clusters of electric lamps revealed a man's figure outlined in the doorway. His eyes traveled about the room as if imploring a nod of recognition, but none was vouchsafed him.

"Collins!" exclaimed Cooper in an undertone.

"Get him!" commanded Fanwell. "Remember, I'm a relation of yours—from the West!"

Hiding his reluctancy, Cooper left his seat and advanced toward the doorway.

"Hello, George!" He extended a hand in greeting.

An expression of drunken amazement overspread Collins's dissipated face. He came forward, almost falling on the other man's shoulders.

"Hello, Tom!" he returned the greeting. "Glad there's one man that ain't ashamed to talk to me. Just look at 'em around here! They act as if they didn't know me. That's a hell of a way to treat a good fellow like me, now ain't it? Just because my name's been in the newspapers!"

Cooper led his friend toward the window.

"Glad to have you join me," he said. "I've got a distant relation here—just in from the West. Wants to see the town."

"Rotten town!" growled Collins. "And the people in it—worse! You're the only good fellow, Tom, I've met all afternoon. Everybody else looked at me like I had a knife out for 'em. Had to drink alone every place I went."

Mr. Fanwell greeted the newcomer cordially, bestowing on him a smile so ingratiating as to put Collins immediately at ease.

"You've probably read a bit about Collins in the papers lately," remarked Cooper.

"Not the Mr. Collins mentioned in connection with the Whitmore case?" asked the detective innocently.

"Yes, that's me!" mumbled Collins. Then, in a burst of drunken unconcern,—"And if you want to turn your back on me too, why, you and Tom may do so!"

"Not at all, not at all!" Fanwell hastened to assure him. "I'm glad to know you. Won't you join us in a drink?"

The invitation seemed to mollify Collins. He smiled foolishly and dropped into a chair. But the cold shrugs, the averted faces which he had met all afternoon still preyed on his mind, and, under the stimulus of a fresh drink, he opened the floodgates of his wrath.

"They're a lot of spineless jellyfish in this town," he drawled. "They all believe I killed Whitmore. Well, I'm not saying whether I did or not. But suppose I did kill him? Ain't a man got the right to defend his home? What's this country coming to when a viper can sneak into another man's house and steal his wife? The papers say that I went around threatening to kill him. Well, I did. And I meant it, too. Why, that yellow cur was sending letters to my wife urging her to leave me. What do you think of that?"

Fanwell and Cooper shook their heads gravely, as if in sympathy with him.

"He dishonored my home!" Collins exclaimed with added vehemence. "He stole my wife—he tried to steal her," he corrected with a sly grin. "And that thieving brother of hers was in sympathy with him! Ever heard of anything like that before? A brother approving the liaison between 'em? And now Ward's bank has busted and I'm ruined! Fine state of affairs—what?"

Collins looked musingly out of the window. He was in a talkative mood, yet Fanwell dared not prompt him into further revelations. To manage a drunken man, or one half-drunk, requires exceptional tact. Once his suspicions are aroused, it is impossible to allay them.

Even now it was evident to the detective that Collins wasn't talking as freely as he pretended to be. He still retained a sufficient amount of caution not to plunge into the details of the murder itself. What he said of his wife's relations with Whitmore was simply a repetition of statements he had made at the club and elsewhere before Whitmore's death. Plenty of witnesses could be obtained who would testify to having heard Collins threaten to kill the merchant. But whether he had actually carried out his threat remained to be proved.

Fanwell was aware that at Police Headquarters opinion as to Collins's guilt was divided. Britz did not believe him guilty, Greig seemed hopelessly befuddled by the conflicting evidence, while Chief Manning dared not venture an opinion. But a majority of the other detectives engaged on the case seemed confident that Collins was the man. Fanwell wondered whether Britz had been led into an error of judgment.

Over Collins a slow transformation was creeping. His eyes, which had blazed indignantly while he was talking, now clouded with a dull mist. The tense expression of his face relaxed and his head sank on his shoulders. He was quickly passing into a state of sodden stupefaction.

Being unfamiliar with Collins's habits and his capacity for drink, Fanwell was trying desperately to think of some means of restoring the drunken man to a condition in which his perverted sense of injuries suffered would inspire his tongue to further revelations.

"Is he a chronic drunk or an occasional drinker?" the detective whispered to Cooper.

"Chronic," came the whispered reply.

"Then he'll recover in a few minutes."

They waited while Collins surrendered completely to the conquering stupor, which seemed more like a heavy sleep brought on by physical exhaustion than the overpowering effect of whisky fumes. His heavy eyelids closed, his jaw hung, he breathed through his mouth. After a time Fanwell shook the unconscious Collins until all the drowsiness left him.

"We're going to dinner," he said. "Come and join!"

Collins waved a repudiating hand.

"Don't want any food," he growled. "Give me a drink."

He was induced to accompany his friends into the dining-room. The smell of food provoked his appetite and he ordered an elaborate meal. When it came he could not eat it. But two or three glasses of champagne revived him temporarily, long enough for him to note the chilling contempt with which the other diners in the room regarded him. After indulging in a long volley of profanity, his mood underwent another change. He grew morose, introspective, self-pitying.

"Nobody cares for me!" he whined. "They've all turned against me. But there's one that would have stood by me—she's dead!"

His memory of her grew suddenly tender and tears filled his bleary eyes.

"She was all right—a good girl but stubborn," he proceeded in a maudlin way. "Got the marriage craze! Wanted me to let my wife get a divorce and marry her! She didn't want to live dishonored all her life. And she killed herself—poor Julia!"

As the name dropped from his lips, Collins bolted upright in his chair.

"I'm going to the flat," he said. "That's where I was happy."

"Wait and we'll go with you," suggested Cooper on a nudge from the detective.

"All right," assented Collins. "You're the only friend I've got left."

They hurried through the rest of the meal, then descended to the lobby of the club. While Cooper and Collins waited for their hats and coats, Fanwell darted into the telephone booth and called up Police Headquarters.

"I've got him roped," he said. "If Britz calls up tell him he's on the way to Julia Strong's apartment."

The bracing night air did not dispel Collins's melancholy. He walked with head bent, a woe-begone expression engraved on his face. At the door of the apartment house in which Julia Strong had killed herself, he hesitated an instant. But, observing that his companions had already entered the vestibule, he overcame his hesitancy and followed them within.

The elevator boy eyed the three men curiously as he took them to the floor on which the apartment was situated. And he lingered inquisitively while Collins inserted the key in the lock and opened the door.

They entered with a vague feeling of gloom, as if about to step into a death chamber. Nor did they regain their spirits on perceiving the disordered condition of the place, with the many mementos of her who had killed herself in fear that she had betrayed Collins, scattered about.

"I wish she was here now," said Collins, tenderly picking up a white glove that had been thrown to the floor. "I might have married her at that!"

The others disposed themselves in chairs while Collins wandered aimlessly about the apartment. Grief-stricken though he was, he showed no appreciation of the significance of the tragedy for which he was in large measure responsible. For an hour he tired his companions with stories of Julia Strong's beauty, of her faithfulness and of her remorse when she realized the full import of her surrender to him.

"But I'm glad they made me stay at home," he declared. "I'd have broken down over her body."

The thought of her cold, lifeless form, recalled to his rum-soaked brain the funeral arrangements that had been made for her.

"That man Luckstone is a great lawyer," he said. "He looked after it all. Had the body shipped home to her parents! They thought she was earning a living here—never knew I was supporting her. Wonderful man—Luckstone! Did it all so quietly, too!"

"Saved you a lot of trouble, didn't he?" Cooper encouraged him to proceed.

The word trouble jarred Collins's train of thought out of its remorseful channel.

"Trouble!" he echoed, raising his voice to a high pitch. "I've certainly got trouble on my hands. But I'm glad she's not here to share it. She wanted luxuries—I gave 'em to her. We'd both be in a fine predicament now, wouldn't we? All my money gone—sunk in Ward's schemes! Oh, they're a fine combination—Ward and my wife!" he declared bitterly. "She thought herself too good for me, too virtuous to remain my wife! You've read of Ward's failure—the papers must be full of it! Well, I'm the one that's hit. All my money, every cent I've got is in his bank. Oh, just wait till I see him!"

He paused, turning an agonized countenance on his friends. The loss of the girl for whom he had provided the apartment had touched his sense of remorse; the loss of his money swept him with an anguish so keen that for the time it excluded all other emotions from his mind.

"We're all paupers!" he exclaimed. "Made paupers by Ward. Ward—yes, damn him! Ward—the thief! My respectable brother-in-law! Ward—the—"

Collins stopped short, amazement written across his features. He stood mute, lips pendent, his eyes bulging forward as if gazing at an apparition. Cooper and Fanwell, following his gaze, beheld the door standing ajar and revealing a man's form with one hand on the knob, the other braced against the jamb. Evidently the newcomer had changed his mind after opening the door, and was about to close it softly, without revealing himself. On being discovered, however, he came forward boldly, shutting the door after him.

With his back against the portal he surveyed the three men in the room, but without a gleam of recognition in his eyes.

"Well—who are you?" brusquely demanded Collins.

"I am Detective-Lieutenant Britz," the visitor said in even tones. "Sit down, Collins!"

CHAPTER XVII

Collins obeyed. Not voluntarily, but because he was unable to resist the domination of the detective's will. Also, a terrible fear had gripped his heart, producing a terror that sobered him and gave him command of all his faculties.

"Who are these men?" inquired Britz, nodding toward Cooper and Fanwell.

"Friends of mine," growled Collins.

"I wish to speak with you, Collins," said the detective. "Do you want them to remain?"

"I do."

"You prefer to have witnesses present?"

"I wouldn't talk to you without them," said Collins.

"But I want to give you an opportunity to explain certain things in connection with Mr. Whitmore's death."

A crafty expression overspread Collins's face.

"Look here, officer!" he exclaimed, a weak smile on his lips. "I'm no boob!" Obviously, he meant this lapse into the slang of the Tenderloin to convey his intimate knowledge of police methods. "You can't soft-soap me! You don't want explanations! You want me to get myself in bad. But you won't get anything out of me. I know my rights."

This defiant speech produced an effect opposite to what Collins had intended. The detective banished the note of persuasion from his voice and adopted an accusing tone, heightened by a manner almost ferocious.

"You don't want to get yourself in bad!" he snarled. "Well, you're in so bad now that you can't possibly get in worse. You threatened to kill Whitmore. You knew that he had discovered your double life! You intercepted the letter which he had sent to your wife."

Collins's pale face had grown paler. So the detective knew of the intercepted letter! Where did he obtain knowledge of it? Only those immediately concerned in the case were aware of its existence. Who had told the police of it?

"What letter are you talking about?" Collins made a bold pretense at ignorance.

"This letter," Britz produced the note which Whitmore had sent to Mrs. Collins.

On seeing the familiar handwriting Collins leaped out of his chair.

"Where'd you get it?" he demanded.

"Sit down!" commanded Britz. "I'll tell you when I get ready. You showed the letter to your wife and she decided to leave you. Then you started forth to kill Whitmore. But he had disappeared. He did not return for six weeks. Then, one day he came back. He was found in his office dead, with a bullet in his body. This is the bullet."

Britz held the leaden pellet between his fingers, then laid it on the table.

"It was taken from Whitmore's body," he explained. "It was fired from a 32-caliber revolver—in fact from this very weapon."

From his coat pocket Britz produced the weapon, a gleaming steel revolver of the hammerless variety.

"Do you recognize it?" he inquired, extending it toward Collins.

Collins's hand did not reach for the weapon. All his confidence had vanished. Fear seemed to paralyze him.

"That isn't all," proceeded the detective with aggravating assurance. "The chambers in this revolver were filled from a box of fifty cartridges. There are five chambers. After the shooting the chambers were emptied and the unused shells returned to the box. Here is the box."

This time Britz offered Collins a small pasteboard box, but Collins shrank from it as if afraid it might explode in his hand.

"You will observe," Britz went on, "that there are forty-nine cartridges left in the box. One is missing—the one that was exploded. Now Collins"—the detective's jaw snapped viciously—"you've decided to remain silent! Well, I've shown you some mute witnesses whose testimony will be understood perfectly by a jury."

All the blood had drained from Collins's face. A violent tremor racked his frame.

"Where'd you get them?" he asked helplessly.

"In your house," answered the detective. "I searched the premises this afternoon."

Collins looked appealingly from the detective to his friends. They had listened to Britz's recital with impassive countenances, and their expressions did not change as they met Collins's gaze.

"What right had you to search my house?" demanded Collins. "I'm not accused of any crime."

"Not yet," agreed Britz. "But the circumstances which I have mentioned may make it necessary for a formal accusation to be lodged against you."

Again Collins displayed remarkable recuperative power. A few moments ago he had seemed on the verge of utter collapse. Now he stiffened with a new accession of courage. Britz, studying this weakling, discerned unmistakable signs that Collins's courage was not drawn from any internal spring. It was communicated to him from without, probably by some dominating mind to whose guidance he had agreed to submit. His strength was continually replenished through reliance on someone in whose judgment he had an abiding faith; a faith that even Britz's convincing recital of condemning circumstances was unable to shake. The detective determined to ascertain who had advised Collins, who had outlined rules for his safe conduct through the tortuous channels into which he had plunged when he announced his intention of killing Whitmore.

"Do you wish to advise with anyone before answering my questions?" asked Britz.

"I won't talk—I won't do anything without the consent of my lawyer."

"Oh, so you've engaged a lawyer!" sneered Britz, as if he interpreted the hiring of an attorney as additional proof of guilt. "Who is he?"

"Mr. Thomas Luckstone." Collins could see no harm in revealing that one of the shrewdest lawyers in the city was looking after his interests.

"And he has advised you to remain silent?"

"I've been around this town long enough to learn the value of silence. Luckstone didn't have to tell me that."

"Well, what's the use of trying to give you a chance?" Britz fired at him. "I've got enough evidence now to convict you. I guess I'll just proceed to lock you up and let Luckstone try to get you out."

Ever since Whitmore's death Collins had been steeling himself for precisely this situation. He was sufficiently experienced in the ways of the world to know that the police investigation must eventually lead to him. This belief was confirmed daily as he read the developments of the case in the newspapers. Soon or late, the police would demand that he explain his conduct. And failure to do so would be fraught with sure consequences.

Britz, silently analyzing Collins's refusal to unbosom himself, concluded that only some extreme measure could drag the truth from his unwilling lips. It was to be seen that life in jail held no allurements for Collins.

Ordinarily he would fight desperately against even temporary detention. That he was ready to submit unprotestingly now, argued an acquiescence in some agreement into which he and the other suspects had entered for mutual safety and protection. Under pressure of third degree methods Collins might falter, but in the end his natural suspicion and dislike for the police, combined with the advice which his lawyer had imparted to him, would prevail over the best efforts of his inquisitors.

At any rate, Britz recognized that the time had not arrived for exerting the full measure of authority over Collins. So he determined to change his tactics, but in a way not to inspire Collins with an exultant sense of victory.

Britz passed a wink to Fanwell, who nodded understandingly. Up to this time no glint of recognition had passed between them, and they were careful to hide their silent signal from Collins.

Ostentatiously, and with some display of temper, Britz removed the revolver and the other exhibits from the table and restored them to his pockets. After which he produced a pair of handcuffs, opening one of the steel bracelets with a sharp click.

"Collins, extend your wrist!" he commanded, thrusting forward the open ring.

Before Collins had time to obey, Fanwell discarded the air of aloofness with which he had watched the proceedings and stepped between the two men.

"This is an outrage!" he exclaimed, addressing Britz. "What right have you to come here and question this man, then arrest him without a warrant? I protest against these proceedings! I won't permit Mr. Collins to submit!"

Britz turned fiercely on him.

"Who are you?" he roared, as if aroused to a burning fury.

"I am a friend of Mr. Collins," returned Fanwell. "I won't permit a friend of mine to be dragged to prison this way."

"Be careful—you are interfering with an officer of the law," cautioned Britz.

"If you arrest him you might as well arrest me too," said Fanwell. "But you won't keep us behind the bars long. I'm from the West, but thank goodness! I have unlimited credit here. I know where to obtain bail—in any amount."

"The charge against this man is murder in the first degree," Britz retorted. "The crime is not bailable."

The information seemed to stagger Fanwell. He bestowed a compassionate glance on the bewildered Collins, then executed a despairing gesture as if he meant to convey that the situation had passed out of his hands.

"Collins, I believe you're innocent. Why don't you speak and clear yourself?" urged Fanwell.

Coming, as it seemingly did, from a disinterested friend, the advice struck Collins with peculiar force. He wavered, and, to encourage his growing desire to talk, Britz withdrew the handcuffs.

"Let me think it over," he pleaded. "Perhaps I may change my mind—and tell you everything."

"Better follow your friend's advice," urged Britz. "He has no self-interest to serve. If you wait to consult with others, they'll only advise you in a way that will best serve their interests, not yours. Don't you think I'm right?" Britz asked Fanwell.

"Yes," came the quick reply.

"What do you think of it?" the detective asked Cooper.

"I'm an old friend of George," he answered. "I should advise him to clear himself at once."

It did not occur to Collins that these three men were playing the same game; that they were ranked in coalition against him. But before his mind there hovered perpetually a vague presentiment of danger, that made him mistrust his own impulse to yield to their urging.

"I can't do it!" he exclaimed despondently. "You wouldn't understand—and you wouldn't believe me."

"If your story is true it ought to be easy enough to furnish proof of it," retorted Britz.

The pitiless baiting to which Collins was being subjected was beginning to tell on him. He turned his poor, befuddled head to one side, then to the other. His eyes shot mute appeals for help, but no answering gleam of compassion came from the others. They regarded him with cold, stolid faces, expressionless as death masks.

"Why can't you leave me alone?" pleaded Collins. "I didn't kill Whitmore."

The denial was uttered in the tone of a fervent plea, but it made no visible impression on the detective.

"If you didn't do it, why don't you establish your innocence?" Britz pursued relentlessly.

"You haven't proved me guilty!" Collins fired back. Evidently something which Luckstone had told him flashed across his mind, for he seemed to come out of his bewildered state, and again he adopted an air of resolute opposition. "I won't say another word."

Britz met this altered attitude of Collins with a swift transformation of his own. His face contracted until every line seemed to harden into an expression of stern determination.

"Do you know why Julia Strong killed herself?" he snapped.

"Yes," said Collins weakly.

"Why?"

"She threatened to do it a dozen times. She wanted me to permit my wife to obtain a divorce so I could marry her."

Collins had been taken off his guard and Britz found it easy to follow up his advantage.

"You promised to marry her?" he inquired.

"I never told her so."

"But you led her to believe you would?"

"I wasn't responsible for what she believed."

"Now I'll tell you something," pursued the detective in a firm, subdued voice. "An hour before Julia Strong committed suicide she was in my office at Police Headquarters."

Collins started as if jarred by a hateful sound.

"I—I—don't believe it," he faltered.

"She was there," said Britz, ignoring the other's remark. "Moreover, she accused you of having killed Whitmore. She did it in the presence of a witness, and, although she was unaware of it, her statement was taken down by a hidden stenographer."

"Then why did she commit suicide?" blurted Collins, as if her death contradicted the detective's statement.

"She betrayed you because you had betrayed her. She thought you and your wife had become reconciled. Then, when she received your note—the one that Beard brought her—she believed you meant, after all, to marry her. In a fit of remorse at having betrayed you, she killed herself."

"Why do you tell me this?" asked Collins suspiciously.

"To show you what an overwhelming mass of evidence we have against you. And to give you a last opportunity to explain."

Collins's eyes traveled about the room, lingering on the various objects that were so intimately associated with the woman whom he had thought so loyal.

"So she too was ready to turn against me!" He shook his head in a self-pitying way. "The one person who, I thought, would never desert me!" His eyes took on a fixity, as if gazing at a distant object. "Money gone!" he murmured, as if talking to himself. "Girl dead—a traitor! Home broken! What's the use?"

The others watched him silently, breathlessly, their eyes lighted with eager expectancy. Collins had sunk into that state of complete despondency wherein even the primal instinct of self-preservation is weakened to the point of extinction. Britz had applied the much-abused and publicly misunderstood third degree in a manner shrewdly calculated to shatter the resisting qualities of the victim's will. By alternately tyrannizing over and cajoling the prisoner—for Collins virtually was a prisoner—he had finally produced in him a condition of mind that invariably leads to confession.

"Well, Collins!" Britz smiled encouragingly. "Only one man can save you—that's yourself. You know as well as I how quickly the others would sacrifice you to save themselves. If you permit them to destroy you, you have only yourself to blame."

Collins lifted his head and met the steady gaze of the detective. The last ounce of resistance had departed from his weak nature. He was ready to yield. But a sudden interruption occurred to divert the attention of those in the room. Someone was banging violently on the door. Britz motioned the others not to leave their chairs, hoping that whoever was seeking admittance would conclude that the apartment was unoccupied and leave. But the banging continued until finally the detective was moved to open the door.

A man burst into the room, brushing past Britz and precipitating his figure into the sitting room.

"Luckstone!" exclaimed Collins, bounding out of his chair.

The lawyer gazed angrily from his client to Britz.

"What does this mean?" he demanded.

"It means that Mr. Collins has dispensed with your services and is ready to confide in me," answered the detective with calm assurance.

Luckstone's eyes narrowed on Collins. The latter nodded a weak assent to the detective's words.

"I've been searching for you all evening," the lawyer burst forth excitedly. "Called up your house, went to the club and finally took a chance on finding you here. I was afraid something like this might happen. I hope you haven't communicated anything to these men."

"Oh, what's the good of remaining silent any longer?" asked Collins surlily.

"What's the good!" repeated the lawyer with a rising inflection. "Do you wish to spoil everything? Do you want to condemn yourself?"

"What!" shouted Collins, now beside himself with rage. "Condemn myself! What do you mean?"

"I mean that if you say a single word, I shall withdraw as your counsel and permit the law to take its course."

"Then you're trying to intimate that I killed Whitmore!" Collins took a step forward, a look of horrified amazement on his face. "So there's a conspiracy now to shift it on to me—eh! Now that I've been robbed and left penniless—"

"You're not penniless," interjected the lawyer. "Your money is intact."

Collins's eyes expanded into an expression of incredulous wonder.

"What are you talking about?" he demanded savagely. "Are you trying to fool me? My money's in Ward's bank—"

"And every creditor will be paid in full," interrupted the lawyer.

"Who's going to pay them?" sneered Collins.

"Your wife."

A loud peal of ironic laughter burst from Collins's lips. But Luckstone silenced the sarcastic merriment with the remark,—

"She has inherited Mr. Whitmore's estate and announced her determination to repay every dollar of her brother's obligations. This police officer,"—he pointed a contemptuous finger toward Britz—"will confirm what I say."

It required no confirmation to convince Collins of something which he was only too eager to believe. And the knowledge instantly repaired his shattered nerves. Before the intrusion of the lawyer, Collins, made dizzy by the multiplicity of incriminating circumstances so adroitly unfolded by the detective, overcome by the rapidity of Britz's blows, was an abject creature ready to surrender his soul. All the enchantment had suddenly passed out of his life, for, to one of his disposition, a liberal income is as necessary as water to a parched plant. Deprived of his fortune, existence wasn't worth while. But with the certainty that his money would be restored to him, life regained all its roseate tints. As the future outlook cleared and he saw that he could return to his indolent mode of living, a sudden reaction took place within him, filling him with a sullen aversion for the detective who had so nearly beguiled him into committing an irreparable breach of faith—if nothing worse. And he turned fiercely on Britz.

"So you tried to entrap me!" he exclaimed with bitter emphasis. "But you didn't succeed, did you? And from now on I shall remain in the hands of Mr. Luckstone, my attorney."

"That is the sensible thing to do," commended the lawyer.

"Why, he threatened to handcuff me and take me to jail if I didn't tell him all about Mr. Whitmore's death," complained Collins.

Luckstone turned to face Britz. He found the detective as imperturbable as though he were but a disinterested spectator in this exciting drama.

"So you had it in mind to make another prisoner?" the lawyer said sneeringly. "You've got Mr. Beard in the Tombs and you have Mrs. Collins at Headquarters—"

"What—he arrested my wife?" Collins asked excitedly. "Is she accused of murder?"

"Calm yourself," the lawyer cautioned him. "This detective is so befuddled he doesn't know whether he's walking on his head or his feet. He's just running around helter-skelter arresting everybody he comes in contact with, regardless of whether he has sufficient evidence or not. In fact, he hasn't any evidence—not a particle against anyone. But he hopes to browbeat somebody into incriminating himself or somebody else—it doesn't matter whom so long as the victim will help the police to make out a case that will justify an indictment by the Grand Jury. Mr. Detective-Lieutenant Britz is on a grand fishing expedition, throwing out bait—"

"You are mistaken," Britz now interrupted the lawyer. "I am not throwing out bait. I am about to draw in my lines, with the fish securely hooked."

CHAPTER XVIII

Collins and the lawyer exchanged questioning glances. What new trick was this detective about to play? The positive tone employed by Britz in announcing that he had hooked his fish, worried them. The provoking coolness of the detective aggravated them beyond measure.

"Evidently you are preparing to draw in a whole netful of fish," said Luckstone experimentally.

"I didn't cast a net," Britz informed him. "I threw out single lines. Do you wish to be present when I draw them in?"

"I shall be glad to be there," the lawyer replied.

"And if Mr. Collins will also promise to be on hand I can save him the discomforts of a Headquarters' cell," said Britz.

"Then Mr. Collins is not the fish you are after?" asked Luckstone.

"You are better acquainted with the game in this criminal aquarium than I am," retorted Britz.

"Well, if you are through with Mr. Collins, I should like a few minutes of private conversation with him," said the lawyer.

"I shall refrain from arresting Mr. Collins only on condition that he remain in custody of one of my men. He may go where he chooses, but only in the company of a detective."

"And if he refuse your condition?"

"Then I shall be compelled to arrest him."

"And multiply the blunders which you have made in this case!" Luckstone smiled sarcastically.

"I am responsible for the conduct of this investigation," snapped Britz. "And let me tell you, Mr. Luckstone, you may think your crafty brain has succeeded in outwitting the police, but it hasn't. From the outset I recognized your handiwork in guiding the various persons concerned in this murder case. You were Whitmore's lawyer! You're Beard's attorney, you're Mrs. Collins's counsel, you represent Collins, and probably Ward also."

"Mr. Ward is my client," acknowledged the lawyer.

"You have fortified them all behind a wall of silence," pursued Britz in even voice. "But the moment I give the signal, the wall will crumble and your clients will simply fall over one another in their desire to talk."

"I shall be interested to see the wizard's wand with which you're going to achieve so much!" Luckstone sneered.

"I promise you that pleasure."

Crossing the room, Britz opened a window and nodded to someone who evidently was waiting in the street. In a few minutes a detective arrived at the door of the apartment and knocked for admittance. Britz invited him to enter.

"Collins, this is Detective Hastings," said Britz in introduction. "You will remain in his custody for the present! Hastings,"—he addressed the detective—"if this man tries to elude you, arrest him and bring him to Headquarters."

Britz left the apartment, an exultant gleam in his eye. The long interview with Collins, even the intervention of Luckstone, had brought him closer to the final unraveling of the absorbing mystery that had developed so many amazing complications. As he hastened toward the subway station, he was fired by a sense of imminent triumph, felt the first happy thrill of approaching victory.

It was no vain boast in which he had indulged before the crafty Luckstone. The detective had been following a carefully devised plan through his investigation, and he was about to reap the fruits of his industry. The Whitmore case would not take rank among the unsolved murder mysteries of the city. In fact, to Britz it was no longer a mystery.

The detective entered Headquarters in a happy frame of mind. He was in control of the situation, had mastered all the complexities of the case.

As he crossed the corridor, passing three or four groups of waiting detectives and policemen, he became aware of an atmosphere of suppressed excitement that seemed to fill the place. The men were talking in low tones, and instinctively Britz guessed that their conversation related to some new turn in the Whitmore case.

Entering the office of Chief Manning, he found the Chief still at his desk. A foot away sat another man, evidently pleading a favor. Britz was about to withdraw, but Manning called him back.

"This is Mr. Lester Ward!" said the Chief.

Britz showed not the least surprise. Nor was he astonished to find Ward at Headquarters. In fact, he had figured that the fugitive banker would return the moment he read the late afternoon papers, which contained an account of the happenings in the banking establishment. The detective argued also that Ward would present himself at Headquarters and demand permission to see his sister.

"So you came back!" Britz greeted him.

"I never ran away," declared Ward. "I had no reason to."

"You were too busy to visit your office, I presume," said Britz.

"It wasn't that. I simply hadn't the courage to face the crowd which I knew would gather. So I went over to Jersey City to wait until the storm had abated somewhat."

"And before leaving, you had one of my men set upon and rendered helpless to follow?"

"I know nothing about that," insisted Ward.

"No, of course not!" Britz retorted.

"Are you the officer in charge of this investigation?" suddenly asked Ward.

"I am."

"Then perhaps you will tell me why you arrested my sister?" Ward spoke resentfully, turning an indignant countenance on the detective.

"I arrested her because the evidence warranted it," Britz returned.

"It is preposterous!" exclaimed Ward. "My sister a murderess! Why, you don't believe that yourself!"

"Then perhaps you will consent to explain the killing of Mr. Whitmore," Britz fired at him.

"I didn't come here to explain," retorted Ward.

"Well, what did you come here for?"

"To demand the release of my sister."

"Only a magistrate may release her," Britz informed him. "And no magistrate will do that in a murder case."

"But you cannot deny me the right to see her," said Ward.

"I can—most emphatically!" Britz corrected him.

"You mean that I am not permitted to speak with my sister?"

"That is precisely what I mean. She may consult with counsel at a reasonable hour of the day. But she may not receive other visitors until she has been committed to the Tombs."

"Do you—do you intend to send her there?" demanded Ward, his anger mounting.

"She will be regularly committed—it is merely a matter of routine."

"But you are making a grave mistake," pleaded the brother. "Isn't there some way of preventing this additional humiliation?"

"There is a way," said Britz calmly.

"How?" inquired Ward eagerly.

"By giving us the full story of Mr. Whitmore's death as you know it."

"But I can't—I'm not at liberty to talk," protested Ward. "I am acting under Mr. Luckstone's instructions."

"I thought so," Britz returned dryly. "So we'll let the law take its course."

"And I'm not permitted to see her to-night?" pleaded Ward.

"No," said Britz curtly. Then, after a moment, he added: "If you will call here at 10 o'clock to-morrow morning, I may convince you of the desirability of acting with the police, instead of against them."

When Ward was out of the room, Britz turned smilingly on the chief.

"I'm about ready for the grand climax," he said.

"That so?"—mockingly from the chief.

"Yes. I've tried all the lines of least resistance," continued the detective, unresentful of the other's aggravating manner. "They led me against a wall of silence. Now I'm going to discharge my heavy ordnance against the wall."

"Got something up your sleeve—eh!" drawled Manning.

"Not up my sleeve—in my mind," said Britz, tapping his forehead. "I wanted to save Mrs. Collins as much notoriety as possible. I could see no use in parading all her domestic troubles before the public. So I gave her a chance to take me into her confidence, but she refused. She, or Collins, or Beard, or Ward, could have saved us all a deal of trouble by breaking silence. Everyone of them knows what we are furiously striving to learn. I addressed myself to each of them individually, tried to obtain enlightenment from each. Now I shall fight them collectively—I'll get the truth, regardless of whom I have to crush in the process of extraction."

The chief shook his head dubiously.

"It looks to me now as if you're all in a muddle. You've got two of them under arrest—why don't you lock up Ward and Collins and have them all in jail? Then you'd be sure to have the guilty party."

"I shall see to it that Beard obtains his liberty to-morrow," was Britz's reply.

"And then what?"

"Then for the grand climax," said Britz.

CHAPTER XIX

The first thing Britz did the following morning was to call the Chief of Police of Atlanta on the telephone.

"Yes, I've arranged for the writ of habeas corpus," said the Atlanta chief in response to Britz's questions. "I've also induced the Federal district-attorney not to oppose the man's discharge. Yes, I also saw the prisoner last night at the jail. He's worried to death that he'll be rearrested and given a long term for aiding Whitmore to escape."

"I've helped the Federal authorities when they required local assistance," replied Britz. "So I feel confident they'll agree to grant him immunity for helping us to solve this murder case. When do you think you can obtain his release?"

"This morning, I hope."

"Then he should be in New York to-morrow morning?"

"Yes."

Next Britz called up the coroner.

"Coroner," he said, "I want you to discharge Beard from prison. Mrs. Collins will be arraigned in Jefferson Market Court this morning and remanded to your custody. She'll have to stay in the Tombs until to-morrow, when I'm going to ask you to continue your preliminary investigation of Whitmore's death. Will you hold court down here?"

"Why all this maneuvering?" inquired the coroner.

"It is necessary," Britz assured him. "We'll solve this case to-morrow, if you help me."

"Very well!" the coroner agreed.

For half an hour Britz devoted himself to the reports of his various subordinates. He learned that Ward had spent the night in his home, while Collins and the detective assigned to guard him, occupied a room in a Broadway hotel. Britz was interrupted in the further perusal of the reports by the doorman.

"Mr. Lester Ward is outside."

"Tell him to wait—and see that he does wait!" directed the detective.

It was a quarter of eleven before Britz was ready to receive his visitor. Ward found the detective with hat and coat on, prepared to leave the building. He had just received a telephone message from one of his men at Delmore Park.

"I'm on my way to the coroner's office," said Britz. "Come along!"

Still dazed by the crowded incidents of the last twenty-four hours, Ward followed the detective to the Criminal Court House, on the ground floor of which the coroner's office is situated. They found Coroner Hart in his private room, engrossed in the routine of his work.

"Just a word, coroner!" Britz called him aside.

The two held a whispered consultation, after which the coroner returned to his desk. Britz and Ward occupied chairs at the farther end of the room, near the window. Half an hour passed, in which neither of them spoke. Presently an attendant entered and whispered to the coroner.

"Bring Horace Beard over from the Tombs!" the coroner said aloud.

Ward began to display signs of uneasiness.

"Must I meet him?" he inquired.

"It won't do any harm," Britz replied.

A moment later the door opened again, and was held ajar by the attendant. Ward tried to avert his gaze from the swinging portal, but his eyes insensibly wandered back to the spot through which his successful rival in love must enter. Suddenly the banker leaped out of his seat and stood stiffly erect, gazing tensely at the attractively slim figure of Josephine Burden.

"Joe!" he called, advancing timorously.

She shrank back toward the door.

"I didn't expect to see you here," he said, halting half a dozen feet from where she stood.

"Where is Mr. Beard?" she inquired, an expression of alarm written on her pale face.

"He'll be here in a minute or two," the coroner informed her. "Sit down!"

She came forward hesitantly and seated herself on the edge of a chair.

"Josephine!" Ward appealed to her. "Don't you see the mess you are getting into?"

"What mess?" she inquired innocently.

"Why—the notoriety!" He edged closer to her chair. "You're mad to come down here! These officers have induced you to come."

"No, I came of my own accord," she said quietly. "I came to see Mr. Beard."

Ward looked anxiously from Britz to the coroner and back again to the detective. They understood the silent appeal of his glance—he was pleading to be let alone with the girl. But they did not see fit to grant his wish.

"This is no time for you to break the engagement," Ward said to her in an undertone. "Why don't you think it over? You've been carried away by sympathy. You've mistaken pity for love."

She shook her head sadly.

"No, I understand the urging of my heart," she answered. "It is useless for us to discuss it."

The conversation ended abruptly with the entrance of Beard. He was escorted into the room by a guard from the Tombs, who placed himself at the prisoner's elbow, prepared to frustrate any sudden break for liberty.

Beard met the eyes of the girl with an expression which the others were able to interpret instantly. Not a word passed between the couple, but their looks sufficiently conveyed their emotions. On beholding Ward, however, Beard gave a low exclamation of surprise, then looked inquiringly at the girl. She had no opportunity to explain her own amazement at finding Ward in the office, for the coroner broke in with the announcement that he had decided to release Beard.

"I am permitting you to go on your own recognizance," he said to the astonished prisoner, "but I shall expect you to hold yourself in readiness to appear here whenever you are wanted."

"I shall be on hand," Beard promised.

"Then you are at liberty to go," the coroner told him.

If Britz expected to witness a hysterical scene between Beard and the girl, he was doomed to disappointment. He had stage-managed Beard's release, and he also had arranged for the presence of Miss Burden and Ward. He had hoped to produce a happy climax, with Ward present as a conflicting factor, to be carried by jealousy into some foolish act that would result in open hostility between him and Beard.

The happy climax, Britz succeeded in producing. But it was a most dignified, genteel, quiet climax. No emotional outburst occurred, no storm of happiness swept the girl or Beard. The joy they felt was not of the wild, unharnessed kind. It was like an internal bath of sunshine, peaceful, radiant, diffusing a quiet happiness about them.

Nor did Ward give any outward sign of being torn by violent emotions. He held his passions in complete subjugation. If he was consumed by jealousy, his conduct did not betray it. Not a word did he utter as the girl linked her arm in Beard's, and, with a flash of gratitude at the coroner, left the office.

"Did you bring me down to witness this?" Ward turned toward Britz.

"Yes," acknowledged the detective.

"Why?" demanded the banker.

"Because I wanted to ascertain whether I was justified in eliminating Mr. Beard as the possible assassin of his employer."

"And have you eliminated him?"

"I have."

"Because of what occurred just now?" inquired Ward.

"Because of what did NOT occur," Britz informed him.

"I don't understand." Ward looked his amazement.

"You'll understand to-morrow," said the detective. "You may go, Mr. Ward," he added. "Your sister undoubtedly has been arraigned in court by now and probably is at the Tombs. The coroner will give you permission to visit her."

Britz walked out of the office and proceeded slowly to Police Headquarters. In the lobby he encountered Greig.

"Come into my office," said Britz. "And ask the chief to come also."

Greig summoned Manning, and the two followed Britz into the room occupied by the detective.

"Sit down and make yourselves comfortable," said Britz, producing a box of cigars and offering it to the visitors. Britz summoned the doorman.

"Don't permit anyone to disturb us!" he said to the attendant.

Lighting a fresh cigar, Britz disposed himself at his desk, and, turning toward Manning and Greig, said:

"I shall now begin to enlighten you with regard to the Whitmore case."

CHAPTER XX

Manning and Greig settled themselves comfortably in their chairs, prepared to listen to a long recital. The extraordinary methods which Britz had pursued in the conduct of the investigation had puzzled and alarmed them. To the chief it had looked as if Britz were running around in a circle, hopelessly bewildered, mistrusting every palpable lead as a new pitfall.

There were reasons for Manning's anxiety. The department could not afford to "fall down" on this conspicuous case. Public interest had increased rather than diminished during the progress of the investigation, and the newspapers had already begun to hint that the Central Office was "bungling the job."

"Chief, I know you've been worried," Britz began, bestowing on Manning a reassuring smile. "But from the outset I realized there was only one way to solve the crime and nothing has developed to change my opinion."

The air of cheerful confidence which the detective wore did not entirely relieve the chief's apprehensions, although it encouraged the hope that perhaps, after all, Britz could save the department from the disgraceful acknowledgment that it had failed in the most sensational murder puzzle which it was called upon to solve in several years.

"We are rapidly approaching the culminating point in the investigation," Britz continued, "and I shall require your cooperation. In order that you and Greig may help intelligently, it is necessary that I confide my plans to you."

"Fire away!" said the chief. "We won't interrupt."

"The greatest obstacle which I have encountered so far has been Whitmore himself," the detective continued. "His influence over the lives of Collins, Mrs. Collins, Ward and Beard, extends beyond the grave. He is responsible for their silence."

"You didn't expect the murderer to come forward and announce himself, did you?" asked the chief ironically.

"Let me proceed in my own way and you'll see what I mean." Britz bent forward in his seat, as if to impress his words more sharply on the minds of his hearers. "Had I accepted the obvious, I should have been compelled to arrest Collins. We have a solid prima facie case against him. He had the motive for the murder. He threatened to kill Whitmore. The pistol with which Whitmore was killed was owned by Collins."

"But how about the opportunity to kill?" interrupted the chief. "Have you established his presence at the scene of the crime?"

"That phase of the case will be developed to-morrow," replied Britz. "Before we get to it let us analyze Collins's position more minutely. He had plenty of time after the shooting to dispose of the weapon and the cartridges. He neglected to do it. It would have required but a minute or two for him to destroy the letter which he intercepted. That letter, the last which Whitmore ever wrote, and the fact that Collins was aware of its contents, could be used by us to establish Collins's motive for the crime. Collins must have known, in fact it was impossible for him to avoid the knowledge, that the police would eventually search his home. Yet he permitted the letter and the pistol and the box of cartridges to remain in his room, where they could not possibly be overlooked. And all the while, it must be remembered, he was in consultation with the astute Luckstone.

"Now what is the inevitable conclusion? Why, he was courting arrest. More than that, he was thrusting evidence on us—evidence which would assure his indictment and trial before a petit jury.

"Do you think he was doing it because he wanted to be convicted? Or do you think Luckstone would have permitted him to leave this evidence lying about except to delude us? Not for an instant.

"No, chief, Luckstone had some design of his own in thus urging us to the conclusion that Collins was the guilty man. But I saw the trap which his crafty brain devised. Luckstone has evidence with which to offset everything we could bring forward against Collins. He planned to make a colossal fool of the prosecution. Being absolutely sure of obtaining Collins's acquittal, he wanted us to proceed with our case against him. He wanted us to commit ourselves to Collins's guilt, to bring Collins to trial, so as to preclude us from proceeding against the real murderer when we ascertained his identity. In other words, he figured that if we declared our belief in Collins guilt and forced him to trial, we'd be glad to drop the case and permit the public to forget it, after Collins was acquitted.

"Did Collins actually commit the murder?" Britz shook his head gravely. "You can bet your last dollar he didn't. In the first place, had he fired the shot, Luckstone would have worked furiously to divert suspicion from him. Every bit of damaging evidence would have been destroyed. It was because Luckstone knew that Collins was innocent that he was willing we should accuse him of the crime.

"Equally convincing is the attitude of the others in the case. You must remember none of them had any use for Collins. Had he shot Whitmore, a chorus of accusations would have gone up instantly. His own wife would have volunteered to become a witness against him. She loved Whitmore and hated Collins. Ward would have denounced him in unmistakable terms. Beard would have been shouting his guilt from the housetops. Far from uniting in a conspiracy to shield him, they would have allied themselves with us to avenge the death of the merchant."

Manning and Greig were listening with faculties intensely alert, carried along by the irresistible course of Britz's logic. They were compelled to acknowledge to themselves that Collins had been effectually eliminated as the murderer. But on whom would Britz fasten the crime?

"Now let us take up Beard," proceeded the detective as if narrating a commonplace happening in the routine of police duty. "He is named in Whitmore's will as one of the executors of the estate. But so is Luckstone! Surely that is no motive for murder. My men have investigated Beard's life. There's nothing in it to discredit him in the least. Moreover, we have ascertained that he was entirely devoted to Whitmore's interests. There was a great personal tie between the two men. The fact that he arranged the plot for Whitmore's escape and the substitution of prisoners, is but additional proof of his loyalty to his employer. We haven't a scintilla of evidence to connect him with his employer's murder."

Manning and Greig exchanged significant looks. Evidently the same question had flashed across their minds. Were Ward and Mrs. Collins in a conspiracy to kill Whitmore?

As if divining what was in their minds, Britz proceeded to answer their unspoken query.

"To attribute the crime to Mrs. Collins or Ward, or to both of them," the detective said, "it is first of all necessary to find a motive. Only one suggests itself. It is that they killed Whitmore to get possession of his estate.

"We must remember that had Whitmore died intestate, neither of them would have obtained a penny of his fortune. So that, in order to establish our motive, it is necessary to prove that they had knowledge of the contents of the will. All the evidence I have gathered tends to contradict that assumption. Not only have we the statement of the lawyer who drew the will, but the actions of Ward and Mrs. Collins subsequent to the murder belie the theory that they had previous knowledge of the disposition which Whitmore made of his estate.

"I know of Ward's frantic efforts to get sufficient money to keep his banking house afloat. And Mrs. Collins's actions after I informed her that she was the chief legatee proved conclusively that she was as amazed as the rest of us to find that Whitmore had enriched her. All the circumstances combine to force us to discard the theory that Ward and Mrs. Collins expected to profit by Whitmore's death.

"With this theory shattered no plausible motive for their participation in the murder remains. If they didn't know the contents of Whitmore's will, then they had every reason in the world for preventing the merchant's death. Ward was praying for his return, so he might plead with him to help him out of his financial scrape. Mrs. Collins's love for Whitmore was intensely genuine, and moreover, it was pure."

Britz paused, noting the bewildered expression on the faces of Manning and Greig. In their eyes the case had taken on a hopeless, desperate aspect. By faultless reasoning Britz had established the presumptive innocence of the very ones among whom he had confidently expected to find the guilty one.

The chief grew visibly disturbed. So this was the end of Britz's maneuvering! Failure appeared to be written in large capitals across the investigation.

"You don't mean to imply that an outsider committed the murder?" Manning blurted.

"Not for an instant," answered Britz. "I have simply been analyzing the evidence as it concerns the four suspects individually. Were there nothing else, I confess we should be compelled to look elsewhere for the assassin. But all the evidence, taken as a whole, leads irresistibly to the conclusion that one of them shot Whitmore. There is not the slightest trace of any outside agency having been employed."

"But if they're individually innocent, how can they be collectively guilty?" demanded the chief.

"You've misconceived my meaning," said Britz. "You know, in a general way, what has been accomplished in the case. So you must be aware of the peculiar actions of all four of the suspects. The fact that they engaged Luckstone to look after their interests argues a guilty knowledge of Whitmore's death. Then, their silence, their fear of saying something that might incriminate one or all of them—it is impossible to reconcile their conduct with innocence! No. When you survey the entire case, you cannot escape the conviction that Whitmore met his death at the hands of one of them."

"But man alive," broke in the chief, "what evidence have you? Why, you're further away from the solution of the crime than when you started."

"Not at all!" Britz assured him. "We're going to solve the case to-morrow morning, in this very room."

Manning and Greig looked at each other in blank bewilderment. In the light of Britz's explanation of the case, his confident assertion could only be regarded as a vain boast. Or was it the expression of a last, flickering hope, to which he clung desperately, like a man staking his last dollar on a thousand-to-one chance?

"What I want you to see clearly," the detective continued, "is the utter futility of trying to discover the murderer through an investigation from the outside. Almost from the outset I realized the utter impossibility of endeavoring to single out the assassin through following the ordinary clues. That's the reason I directed the entire investigation along a single line—the only line that could possibly lead to success."

The faces of Manning and Greig grew more clouded. They could comprehend the reasoning which cleared the suspects, but they were unable to understand by what contradiction of logic Britz meant to upset his own conclusion.

"Let me make myself clear to you," Britz proceeded. "Such evidence as we have, or such as we might be permitted to present to a jury, all tends to establish the innocence of Mrs. Collins, Ward and Beard. On the other hand, it gives a guilty aspect to Collins's conduct. Yet I am convinced that Collins did NOT do the shooting, while one of the others did.

"There is only one way in which we can single out the murderer. I have found that way."

To the two listeners Britz's statement sounded almost like a confession of failure. It was an indirect admission that he had not learned the identity of the murderer—that he had nothing on which to base a direct accusation.

"We've got to break their silence!" Britz exclaimed impressively. "As long as they remain mute, they are safe. But I've found the way to make them talk—I know where their interests conflict and to-morrow I shall bring them in violent conflict with each other. The result is inevitable."

It was plain from their expressions that Manning and Greig did not share Britz's confidence. They could foresee only disaster. And in the state of nervous depression in which they found themselves they were unable to offer a word of encouragement to the detective. But Britz did not require their encouragement, his own self-confidence being sufficient to sustain him.

"Keep alert to every advantage to-morrow," he enjoined them. "You'll catch what I'm doing and I want you to add emphasis to everything I do and say."

As Manning and Greig were about to depart, Britz made a final effort to dispel the gloomy forebodings that possessed them.

"Don't look so glum!" he said, laying a reassuring hand on their shoulders. "We can't lose. Not only are there grave conflicting interests among them, but I shall invoke against their silence an all-conquering force—the most potent force in all human conduct."

"What is it?" asked Manning and Greig eagerly.

"Love."

CHAPTER XXI

Both Britz and Manning were skilled in the art of concealing their emotions. Their brains might be working furiously, their hearts throbbing with excitement, they might be laboring under the greatest stress of mind, yet they were able to command a placid exterior, unruffled as polished ivory.

Their conduct as they entered the Police Headquarters the following morning gave no suggestion of the strain which they were undergoing. Their faces reflected none of the anxious expectancy with which they looked forward to the enactment of the great climax in the Whitmore case.

But the trained newspaper man, as well as the skilled police officer, is endowed with a peculiar instinct by which he seems to detect, without apparent reason, the presence of impending excitement. He seems to smell it in the air. So that even before Britz began issuing instructions to his men and sending them scurrying out of the building, the reporters at Police Headquarters appeared to know that something of the utmost importance was about to transpire.

That it concerned the Whitmore case became evident when Mrs. Collins was escorted to the building and ushered into Britz's office. She was followed in a few minutes by Collins, Ward and Beard, all of whom had been summoned by Britz.

Next, Luckstone was seen to jump out of an automobile and tear up the steps as if afraid that his ultimate fate depended on the moments required to reach his clients. Finally Coroner Hart entered the building, and was immediately accosted by the reporters.

"What's coming off?" they inquired.

"I don't know myself," he said truthfully. "Britz seems to think something's going to happen."

It was ten o'clock precisely when Britz, Manning, Greig and the coroner passed from the chief's office into the room in which the suspects in the Whitmore mystery were gathered. They found Luckstone in command of the situation.

"What does this mean?" he demanded, advancing toward Britz's desk.

"It means that the coroner is about to resume his preliminary inquiry into the death of Herbert Whitmore," the detective informed him.

"And have I been summoned here as a witness or as counsel to the accused?"

"As counsel, of course," said Britz.

"Then as the attorney for Mrs. Collins and as the legal adviser of the other witnesses I wish to inform you that this proposed examination is utterly useless. I have instructed my clients not to answer any questions."

Britz's eyes swept the faces of the witnesses in a look of sharp scrutiny. He found Mrs. Collins outwardly composed. The dark rings about her eyes betrayed a night of sleeplessness, but otherwise she looked as fresh as if she had just stepped out of her private boudoir, instead of a narrow, stuffy cell in the woman's wing of the Tombs. Evidently she had prepared herself for a great test and had summoned all the stubborn courage of one resigned to suffering, yet who meant to hide her agony from the eyes of the world.

Of the others, Collins appeared to be the most uneasy. He looked almost frightened. From time to time his gaze fixed itself on the face of his wife, but she kept her eyes averted. Only a slight constraint of manner exposed Ward and Beard's diminishing self-control.

"Since the witnesses have been cautioned to remain silent," said Britz, addressing the coroner, "and as they appear resolved to stay mute, we cannot escape the conviction that they have knowledge of the circumstances surrounding the murder of Mr. Whitmore. At present Mrs. Collins is the only prisoner. She is accused as an accessory to the crime. We have ample evidence to establish our case against her. We know of her relations with the deceased. We know, furthermore, that the failure of her brother's bank spelled financial ruin for her, for Collins and for Ward. All three must have been aware that the failure was imminent—that it was inevitable. So Collins, pretending that the sanctity of his home had been violated, went around threatening to kill Whitmore. Of course, it was a shallow pretense, designed to conceal the conspiracy between him, his wife and Ward to obtain possession of Whitmore's estate. We have the weapon with which Whitmore was killed. We have fastened its ownership on Collins. The evidence against him is sufficient to send him to the electric chair. We also have ample evidence with which to convict Mrs. Collins and Ward as accessories after the fact—the law is very plain concerning the concealment of evidence. But I am about to lay a graver charge against them. I have a letter written by Ward in which he implores Whitmore to extend financial assistance to him. Mrs. Collins joined in writing that letter, and, moreover, after the murder, I found her in Beard's home endeavoring to obtain possession of the note. With that letter and other evidence which I have gathered, I am prepared to accuse Mrs. Collins and Ward as accessories *before* the fact. Against Collins I am ready to present a charge of murder in the first degree."

The accused persons looked gravely at their lawyer. But he remained entirely unperturbed, not even vouchsafing a mild protest against the detective's direct accusations.

It was the coroner who broke the silence.

"Then as I understand it," he said, "you wish me to commit Collins on a charge of first degree murder, and Mrs. Collins and Ward as accessories before the fact?"

"Precisely," answered the detective.

"Of course, I don't want to take so drastic a step unless I am compelled." The coroner shook his head dubiously. He had been primed by Britz and was following the part which he had been directed to play. "As the evidence stands, I can see no other course to pursue. But I'm not going to commit anyone on such a terrible charge simply because the police request it. Nor shall I ask Mrs. Collins, Collins or Ward a single question, for anything they say may be used against them. But if Mr. Luckstone cares to present any facts tending to establish the innocence of the accused, I am ready to listen and to give due consideration to anything that he might offer."

The judicial attitude adopted by the coroner surprised and gratified the lawyer. Evidently here was a conscientious official who was not to be precipitated into hasty action at the behest of the police.

"Coroner," said the lawyer, moving his chair forward, "this police officer has been endeavoring to create an atmosphere of guilt about my clients. But in this age prosecutors are compelled to offer something more substantial than atmosphere on which to base their accusations. I realize fully the gravity of the situation as regards my clients. They are absolutely innocent and there will be no difficulty in establishing their innocence before a jury. But we are not anxious to proceed to a public trial, with all the useless suffering which it must entail. In my experience before the bar I have found coroners and committing magistrates invariably predisposed toward the police. They will commit on the flimsiest kind of evidence, content to leave the judicial determination of the case to the higher courts. But the law invests you with a wide discretion in homicide cases. And if you are prepared to scrutinize the evidence carefully before accepting the accusations made by Lieutenant Britz, then I believe I can convince you in short order how absolutely baseless his charges are."

"I have no desire to commit an innocent man or woman to prison," answered the coroner. "I am not an agent of the police. I am a judicial officer and as such I am prepared to protect the innocent to the limit of my powers."

Britz had so arranged the chairs in his office as to compel those in the room to resolve themselves into two separate groups, like opposing sides in a judicial proceeding. Behind the detective's flat-top desk sat the coroner, while about him were ranged Britz, Manning and Greig. Facing the desk, at a distance of a dozen feet, sat Mrs. Collins, Ward, Beard and Collins, with Luckstone occupying a chair in the middle.

The sincerity of tone in which the coroner expressed his willingness to consider the evidence of both sides, encouraged the lawyer to proceed.

"Mr. Whitmore was found dead in his office at the hour when his clerks prepared to go to lunch," he began, in the tone of an advocate addressing a high tribunal on a question of law, rather than of fact. "It has been established beyond question that he arrived at his office between nine and ten o'clock, and that he did not leave his office all morning. It is also a matter of common knowledge that he had no visitors that morning, and the twenty or thirty clerks in the outer office have all sworn that they heard no shot fired and saw no one enter or leave Mr. Whitmore's private room. Now I do not pretend to offer any explanation as to how Mr. Whitmore was killed. But I do maintain that the accusing police officer should be asked to tell how the alleged murderer got to his victim."

"I am not prepared to go into that as yet," Britz interrupted.

"But you mean to imply that you have a satisfactory explanation to offer?" questioned the lawyer.

"That phase of the case gives me no concern," Britz replied curtly. "It is a minor feature of this investigation."

A shade of anxiety passed over the lawyer's face as he noted the coolness with which the detective dismissed what was generally regarded as the most puzzling feature of the entire case. It occurred to him, however, that the detective might be indulging in the favorite police game of bluff—that his easy dismissal of one of the most important features of the mystery was but a sham, a pretense designed to cover his ignorance.

"If you regard the matter so lightly, why don't you disclose your knowledge to the coroner?" he taunted the detective.

"Perhaps he has already done so," the coroner interjected. "At any rate it is self-evident that somebody *did* get to Whitmore and that Whitmore was killed by a bullet wound."

"Very well," said the lawyer, accepting the suggestion. "It is none of my affair, nor does it concern my clients, how the assassin managed to enter and leave Mr. Whitmore's office without being seen by the clerks. The point is, that Collins wasn't within fifteen miles of Mr. Whitmore's office on the day Mr. Whitmore was found dead. And the same circumstance of remoteness from the scene of the crime, absolves Mrs. Collins, Mr. Ward and Beard from participation in the crime."

The lawyer shot an exultant glance at Britz, a glance that adequately conveyed the conviction that he had shattered the entire case against his clients.

Coroner Hart glanced inquiringly from Britz to Chief Manning, as if waiting for some cue.

"Does Mr. Luckstone mean he's got an alibi for all his clients?" Manning said experimentally.

"You caught my meaning precisely." The lawyer smiled confidently at the officials. "Moreover, Mr. Coroner, I shall not hesitate to disclose the nature of our alibis. The police may investigate them and we shall lend all the assistance in our power."

"Of course, there can be no better defense than an alibi," commented the coroner.

"Here are the facts," Luckstone proceeded eagerly. "On the day of the crime, Mr. Collins did not leave his home. Neither did Mrs. Collins. All the servants will bear us out in that. But we have other disinterested witnesses who called at Mrs. Collins's house at various times during the morning and who saw both Mr. and Mrs. Collins in the house. There is the employé of the lighting company who came to read the electric meter, two employés of a vacuum cleaning company whose names you may have, and the canvasser for a magazine who came to solicit a subscription. I have no hesitancy in giving you their names, so you may question them privately.

"As for Mr. Ward and Mr. Beard, their alibis are equally strong. Mr. Ward took the eight-twenty train at Delmore Park, as was his daily custom. He was seen by the station agent and the conductor. Moreover, seven other residents of Delmore Park were in the same coach, and all of them are prepared to testify in Mr. Ward's behalf. His movements after arriving at Grand Central Station fortunately came under the observation of disinterested witnesses. He rode downtown with two of his Delmore Park friends, and one of them accompanied him to the door of the bank. All the employés of the institution are prepared to testify that Mr. Ward did not leave his office until two o'clock."

The lawyer paused to note the impression of his words on the coroner. That official was listening intently, fully cognizant of the weighty import of the attorney's statement.

"Is it necessary to supply an alibi for Mr. Beard?" Luckstone inquired, as if under the impression that the secretary had been eliminated from the case.

"If he has one you may as well outline it," the coroner replied.

The lawyer complied without further urging.

"Mr. Beard spent the entire morning in the vaults of a safety deposit company whose name Lieutenant Britz already has. He was at all times under the observation of the company's watchman."

With the air of one who has succeeded in establishing his case beyond possibility of doubt, the lawyer sat down. The faces of the coroner, the chief and Greig were cast in an expression of grave apprehension. The frankness with which Luckstone had revealed the evidence on which he based his alibis could leave no doubt that the witnesses would confirm all he had said. And against such a downpour of disinterested evidence the police could not hope to sustain their case.

Britz had listened to Luckstone's recital with impassive countenance. Now, however, it was to be observed that the lines about his mouth tightened, that his forehead contracted, while his eyes darted points of fire.

"Do you want to investigate their alibis?" asked the coroner.

"No," snapped Britz.

"Why not?"

"Because it isn't necessary."

"Then you accept them?"

"Yes—without question."

"But if none of the accused was within miles of Whitmore's office on the morning in question, how do you connect any of them with the actual commission of the crime?"

Britz rose and took up a position at the side of the desk, where he could see every fleeting emotion that might cross the faces of all the others in the room. His form stiffened to military erectness, his face took on the purposeful aspect of a man about to carry to fruition plans which he had long nourished in secret. And as the others gazed on him, the conviction forced itself on them that here was a man who would pursue whatever course he had in mind, pitilessly, relentlessly, through whatever wilderness of lies and deceit it might lead. A cold silence fell on them, as if they had been suddenly chilled by the frigid attitude of the detective.

"Coroner, the alibis which Mr. Luckstone presented are worthless," the detective said in a subdued voice that nevertheless penetrated his hearers like an icy wind.

"You mean they are manufactured?" blurted the coroner.

"No—they are true. But they have no bearing on the murder."

"What!" The coroner shot a searching glance at Britz. "If none of the suspects was at Whitmore's office, how could any of them have killed Whitmore?"

"Mr. Whitmore was not killed in his office," said Britz firmly. "He was shot the night before."

CHAPTER XXII

The words came like a stunning blow where a verbal counter-argument was expected. Luckstone and his clients sat like beings who felt the ground slipping from under them, yet were helpless in the paralyzing fear that had seized them. The coroner's eyes traveled from Britz to Manning and Greig, as if seeking confirmation of the detective's statement. But he found only amazement written in their features.

Coroner Hart was the first to recover from the surprise occasioned by Britz's revelation. He became aware of a growing skepticism that refused to accept so obvious an explanation of the puzzling circumstances surrounding the merchant's death. Surely the same solution would have suggested itself to him ere this were it possible for twenty hours to have elapsed between the time of the shooting and the discovery that Whitmore was dead!

"If Whitmore was shot the night before, then he must have deliberately chosen his office in which to die!" the coroner said in disparagement of Britz's contention. "Why, it's impossible! I should have detected it the moment I saw the wound."

Britz now produced the enlarged photograph of the wound as well as the needle that he had found on the floor of Whitmore's office.

"It is all very simple—so simple that I eliminated the theory that Whitmore was killed in his office at the very outset of the investigation. The very preparations that were made to delude us contained the evidence of their own clumsy manufacture. Look at the photograph of this wound!" Britz held the photograph edgewise on his desk. "Do you observe the perforations about the edge of the wound? They tell the whole story. That wound had been sewed up and was opened again with this needle." He held up the slim, steel darning needle to the light.

"But why—why should he do this?" broke in the coroner. "It must have been torture!"

"It was," Britz agreed.

"But the loaded pistol on his desk—how do you explain that?"

"I repeat, Whitmore was shot the night before," replied Britz. "It was a mortal wound. The spleen had been penetrated and he was beyond the aid of medical science.

"The doctor that was summoned undoubtedly told him he was doomed. There was no way to stop the internal bleeding, but the patient might live anywhere from twenty-four to seventy-two hours. We are all familiar with the uncertainties of gunshot wounds—the medical records overflow with cases of wonderful endurance shown by persons suffering from pistol wounds.

"Now what did Whitmore do? Why, he decided to conceal the evidence of his own murder. He instigated the conspiracy to shield his murderer. Moreover he determined to make it appear that he had committed suicide. So he went to his office in the morning armed with the pistol and the needle. It was unquestionably his intention to fire a second shot into the wound but first it was necessary to open it and he did so at great pain. He died, whether from shock or weakness, before his hand was able to reach the pistol on his desk. Had he been able to accomplish what was in his mind, his clerks would have heard the shot, the authorities would have found the pistol and the conclusion of suicide would have been accepted without question."

"Did you see the physician who attended him?" interjected the coroner.

"Yes," replied Britz, "but I couldn't get a word out of him, and under the law I could not force him to tell."

"But the clothing—his underwear would have shown where the blood had dried," the coroner declared.

"Whitmore attended to that," replied Britz. "The moment he opened the wound he permitted the fresh blood to stain the underwear. You see, with the exception of his overcoat he wore the same clothing he had on when he was shot."

Having established the time when the assassin fired the bullet into Whitmore's body, Britz laid aside the picture and the needle and turned savagely on Luckstone.

"Now, sir!" he exclaimed, bringing his fist down on the table. "That disposes of your alibis! You had arranged them very craftily after the shooting—all four of your clients spent the morning where disinterested witnesses could see them. The very fact of their being compelled to supply themselves with alibis proves their guilty knowledge of the crime."

Luckstone was too experienced an attorney not to be prepared to meet any new turn which the case might take. Besides, the coroner's attitude seemed to be antagonistic to the police, and the lawyer resolved not to abandon hope of having the entire matter disposed of at the present hearing.

"It doesn't matter a particle to my clients when Mr. Whitmore was shot," he said, adopting an attitude of indifference. "Since I have entered on a defense, I might as well proceed with it and end the terrible uncertainty and annoyance which they have suffered."

The lawyer left his seat and stood facing Britz, ready to meet any new evidence which the detective had to offer.

"This is what occurred on the night before Mr. Whitmore's death," he proceeded. "Mr. Whitmore arrived home after a long business trip. He communicated with Mrs. Collins and was informed that she, her husband, Ward and Miss Burden had engaged a box at the opera. They went to the opera that night. Miss Burden will bear us out in that. During the first act Mr. Beard joined the party and toward the end of the performance, Mr. Whitmore arrived.

"On leaving the opera house, Mr. Whitmore separated from the others. Collins, Mrs. Collins, Ward and Miss Burden returned to Delmore Park in the Collins machine. Beard accompanied them and spent the night with Mr. Ward. Mr. Whitmore slept in Mr. Beard's home that night. Now what becomes of your theory that Mr. Whitmore was shot by one of my clients? Miss Burden was with them before, during, and after the performance."

Here was another alibi, more potent than the others. For it was evident that if Whitmore was shot after the performance at the opera house, none of the four suspects could be adjudged guilty of the crime. And it was unlikely that Luckstone would have revealed as much as he did unless he were absolutely sure of his ground. Miss Burden and the chauffeur were witnesses whose testimony it would be impossible to shake.

To the coroner it looked as if all four of those before him had absolved themselves from participation in the crime. In fact it would require only the formal testimony of the witnesses named by Luckstone to insure their acquittal.

"You say that Mr. Whitmore returned from a business trip?" asked Britz.

"Yes," answered Luckstone.

"That is untrue." The detective's jaw snapped viciously.

"What do you mean?" An angry flush suffused the lawyer's cheeks.

"I know precisely where Mr. Whitmore spent his time."

As if to avoid further controversy, Britz nodded to Greig and the latter left the room. He returned after a moment accompanied by a man who, for some reason, was trying desperately to hide behind the detective's broad back. Evidently he had no relish for the rôle which he was to play in this tense drama.

"Travis, step forward!" commanded Britz.

The newcomer stepped into the center of the room, a timorous, shrinking figure, pale and haggard. At sight of him Luckstone gave a half-startled gasp. A violent tremor traveled down Beard's frame. The agitation of the lawyer and the secretary extended in milder form to the others in the room.

"Travis, look around this room and see if you can identify the man that hired you to impersonate Herbert Whitmore!" said Britz.

Travis's gaze wandered from face to face, finally fixing itself on Beard's drawn features.

"That is the man!" he said, pointing a trembling forefinger at the secretary.

"That is all!" Britz dismissed him.

This dramatic interruption of the hearing served to increase the strained expectancy with which those in the room had followed the proceedings. A dozen times Manning and Greig had experienced a darting sense of alarm as Britz's case threatened to collapse. Momentarily they expected to hear him acknowledge that he had erred in his accusations and to see him abandon his efforts to fix the crime on Mrs. Collins, Collins, Ward and Beard.

But with each new setback Britz became all the more determined. And now he favored Luckstone with an exultant gleam that carried no hope of compromise.

"You realize the significance of the identification, don't you?" Britz inquired with exasperating coolness.

"I don't see what it has to do with the murder," Luckstone retorted. "My clients never saw Mr. Whitmore after they left him at the opera house."

"Then you mean to intimate that if he was shot that night, the shooting was done by an outsider?"

"That is the only reasonable inference."

"It is a most unreasonable inference," said Britz.

"Why?"

"Because it does not explain why Mr. Whitmore should have tried to give his death the aspect of suicide. Moreover, had he been shot by an outsider, the police would have been notified at once. As a final reason for discarding any theory that he was shot by someone outside of the four persons whom you represent, I mention the silence which they have so consistently maintained."

"They have done so by my advice," said the lawyer.

"And do you still advise them to remain silent?"

"I do, except as to proving an alibi."

"You deem that sufficient?"

"I do. It is all that would be required before a jury."

"I suppose that you have effectually silenced the physician who attended Mr. Whitmore," said Britz, "and I know that the servant in Mr. Beard's house was permitted to spend the night in question with his parents in Newark. So there is nothing left but to ask Mr. Beard to tell us who killed Mr. Whitmore."

CHAPTER XXIII

Thus far Britz, Luckstone and Coroner Hart had occupied the center of the stage. To them had fallen all the speaking parts. The others had played silent roles, but now one of them was suddenly called to participate actively in the drama. He failed to respond.

Beard, far from embracing the opportunity to enlighten the coroner, clung all the more desperately to silence. And in this attitude he was encouraged by a nod from Luckstone.

"Beard, you have nothing to hide," urged Britz. "Why don't you talk? Are you going to aid the murderer of your employer to escape punishment?"

But Beard was not to be enticed into speech. Britz might as well have appealed to a lay figure for all the response he received.

The detective whispered to Greig, who hastened out of the room. Not a word was uttered while he was gone. But a sharp exclamation of protest escaped from Beard's lips when Greig opened the door and deferentially showed a young woman into the room.

"Miss Burden—who brought you here?" demanded Luckstone, bolting out of his chair.

"A detective came for me," she answered in a low voice.

Evidently the summons to appear at Police Headquarters had puzzled her, for she looked in a bewildered way from one to the other of the groups in the room. With a woman's sure instinct, however, she read that something was transpiring which threatened ill to the man who had won her affections, and she walked over to him with hand extended.

"Here is a chair for you," said Britz, halting her. At the same time he placed a seat for her next to Mrs. Collins. An expression of pity overspread the girl's face as she beheld the lines of suffering in the other woman's countenance, and, as she dropped into a chair provided for her, her hand stole into Mrs. Collins's palm.

"Why—what does this mean?" she asked timorously, lifting her eyes to meet Britz's glance.

"Simply that you have been invited here as a witness," the detective replied. "Mr. Beard is going to clear the mystery surrounding Mr. Whitmore's death. He's going to tell us who killed his employer."

"Not a word!" cautioned Luckstone.

"Beard, I'll make your position clear to you!" said Britz dryly. "I'll let you know precisely where you stand. You're keeping silent in a mistaken effort to shield Mrs. Collins from scandal. You're mute for the same reason that Mr. Whitmore tried to hide the fact that he was murdered! He thought he could keep Mrs. Collins's name out of the newspapers. He wanted to save her from scandalous references involving her character! But you see how futile all his efforts were! You see how useless his self-inflicted torture was! Beard, look at this girl!" Britz pointed dramatically toward Miss Burden. "You're engaged to her. You've got a great deal to look forward to! But unless you get up now and tell the truth, the whole truth, concerning Mr. Whitmore's death, I promise you that the next ten years of your life shall be spent in the Federal prison at Atlanta."

Beard shot a look of appeal at Luckstone, but the lawyer remained unmoved.

"You're making a rash promise, officer!" Luckstone scoffed.

"Beard!" Again Britz addressed himself to the frightened secretary. "You've committed a grave crime. You brought about the escape of a Federal prisoner—a man convicted of a serious offense. You've been identified in this very room as the person who engineered the substitution of prisoners. The man Travis will testify against you. But I also have corroborative evidence of his story. There was a trust fund of a hundred thousand dollars established for him. You arranged for that—I have it from the officers of the trust company to whom you went. Moreover, Mr. Luckstone drew up the deed of trust. He may not have committed a criminal offense, but certainly the Bar Association will be interested sufficiently to inquire into his conduct. Now Beard, I'm not working for the Federal government! But I have aided the Washington authorities in many cases and they'll grant any reasonable request which I may make. I feel safe in promising you immunity for arranging the escape of Mr. Whitmore—but you've got to stand up now and tell the truth."

"I can't!" Beard moaned. "I'm pledged!"

"Ten years in prison!" Britz baited him. "Think of Miss Burden! Instead of a happy marriage—the prison stripes! And I promise that you'll get the limit!"

Miss Burden was on her feet, one hand extended imploringly toward Britz.

"You don't mean he'll have to go to prison?" she faltered.

"For ten years!" Britz impressed it on her mercilessly. "Unless they'll"—his hand swept the semi-circle in which the others were seated—"release him from his pledge."

Miss Burden's distress had made a profound impression on everyone in the room.

"Won't you save him?" she pleaded.

A moment's silence was broken by Mrs. Collins. She lifted herself slowly out of her seat, and, bracing herself with one hand against the top of the chair, stood for a tense second facing Luckstone.

"Let Mr. Beard tell!" she said.

The words had an electrical effect. Manning, Greig, Coroner Hart leaned excitedly over the desk. Beard was already on his feet, eager to end the distressing situation. Collins and Ward also left their chairs and advanced toward Britz.

"I'll tell the story!" volunteered Ward.

"No you won't!" interposed Collins. "I'll give my version of it."

"Officer, I have nothing to hide! I'll tell the circumstances precisely as they occurred," Ward repeated.

"No he won't!" protested Collins. "Let me speak! I'm willing to swear to everything I say."

It was almost ludicrous to behold the utter demoralization into which Luckstone's clients were thrown. Britz had brought them out of their coverts and forced them into the open—and instantly they started fighting among themselves.

Luckstone made one ineffectual effort to re-unite them in solid rank against the attacking police enemy, then he also surrendered.

"Let Beard talk!" he exclaimed. "He may be able to save himself from an awful predicament."

"Sit down, gentlemen!" Britz said, as he motioned them to their seats. "I'll hear what Mr. Beard has to say."

CHAPTER XXIV

Beard began to speak, but the tremor of overmastering excitement in his voice, made his words indistinct, incomprehensible. Not until he had proceeded for several minutes did he regain control of his voice, and then he had to repeat what in his agitation he had but half-uttered.

"I met Mr. Whitmore when he left the train at Philadelphia after the substitution of prisoners had been achieved," Beard said. "We proceeded to New York, arriving here about three in the afternoon. I knew that Ward and Mrs. Collins were extremely anxious to see Mr. Whitmore, and he likewise was aware of it. So I telephoned Mrs. Collins and her brother to come to my home.

"As a precautionary measure, Mr. Whitmore had decided to stay at my house until the mustache which he had shaved off was restored to his lip. He thought it best not to appear in the streets as there was grave danger of meeting one of the officials with whom he had come in contact after his arrest.

"Evidently Collins was at home when Mrs. Collins received my message asking her to come to my house. She and Ward arrived there about five o'clock. It was already dark and I switched on the electric lights.

"They met Mr. Whitmore in the library. The greetings were most cordial. Then Ward began to recite his business troubles. He had proceeded only a few minutes when the door-bell rang. I responded and Collins forced his way into the house. Hearing voices in the library upstairs, he darted up the steps and burst in on Mr. Whitmore. Collins had been drinking—just enough to make him ugly. As I entered the room I heard him up-braiding Mr. Whitmore and with each word he grew more excited. Finally he called Mr. Whitmore a vile name. Then Mr. Whitmore opened up on Collins.

"'You cur!' Mr. Whitmore shouted. 'You've been unfaithful to your wife—you betrayed the other woman! You lied to both of them! You made the other woman believe you intended to marry her, and made her your mistress! She's been your mistress over three years now, pleading and imploring that you keep your promise. You've wrecked two lives and now you have the hardihood to come here and accuse your wife—why, you're so low and vile and worthless—'

"'Cut that out!' Collins broke in. 'I want an explanation of this letter!'

"Collins waved the letter which he had intercepted, but Mr. Whitmore tried to dismiss him with a shrug of disgust. Finally Collins repeated the vile epithet which he had called my employer. Then he hurled another epithet at his wife. That enraged Mr. Whitmore and he leaped for Collins. Collins jumped back and whipped out a pistol. At the same instant Ward hurled himself at Collins. In order to prevent a tragedy I switched out the light. There was a short scuffle in the darkness, then a shot rang out. I heard Mr. Whitmore groan.

"Instantly I switched on the light. Mr. Whitmore was leaning against a table, one hand pressed against his abdomen. Collins was cowering against the opposite wall.

"The pistol was in Ward's hand."

Beard paused, overcome by the crushing pain of the memories that crowded on his brain. The fact that all but one of the participants in the tragedy were present now, made the anguish all the more acute.

"I helped Mr. Whitmore into a chair," Beard proceeded in a sobbing voice. "And I heard him say, 'Well, I guess I'm done for!'

"Mrs. Collins then came over and threw her arms about his neck, kissing him and imploring him not to die. Ward joined the group, and with tears running down his cheeks, said:

"'I fired the shot. But I meant to kill that dog'—pointing to Collins. 'I meant to avenge the insult to my sister. I hope the wound won't prove serious.'

"There is no doubt that Ward had wrenched the pistol out of Collins's hand and meant to kill him. But Mr. Whitmore also had tried to get the weapon. And in the darkness there was a mix-up in which Collins managed to slip away after he lost the weapon. When Ward fired, the bullet struck Whitmore. That is the truth of the matter," Beard added imploringly.

Mrs. Collins had buried her face in her handkerchief. She was sobbing convulsively. Miss Burden also was crying, but silently. The coroner and the police officials had hung breathlessly on each word uttered by Beard. Everything he said had carried conviction. His manner was straightforward and he had the bearing of a man deeply moved but striving furiously to retain his self-control.

"What occurred after that, Lieutenant Britz has guessed pretty accurately," Beard continued in a voice of diminishing strength. "I sent for Mr. Whitmore's personal physician. He dressed the wound and told Mr. Whitmore he could not live more than forty-eight hours. Mr. Whitmore had remained conscious all the time, and when he learned there was no hope for him, he showed the most remarkable self-possession I have ever seen a human being display.

"'We must hide the scandal!' he said. 'The doctor will remain with me. I want all you folks to go home and act as if nothing had occurred. To-night, I want you to go to the opera—all of you.'

"Mrs. Collins and Ward protested but Mr. Whitmore insisted that he be obeyed to the letter. And he sent me home with the Collinses and Mr. Ward to see that his orders were carried out.

"Oh, it was a delightful opera party that night!" A wan smile appeared on Beard's face at the recollection of it. "While we were gone Mr. Whitmore consulted with Mr. Luckstone. I have no personal knowledge of what transpired between them, but I presume that Mr. Luckstone outlined the plan which was subsequently followed and by which it was meant to establish an alibi for everyone present at the shooting.

"At any rate, Mr. Whitmore appeared in our box at the opera toward the end of the performance. He must have been suffering terribly, but he hid his sufferings from us. While I didn't know it then, I know now that he appeared at the opera in order to make it seem that he must have been shot sometime after he parted from us.

"I believe the doctor remained with him all night. In anticipation of Mr. Whitmore's homecoming I had sent the servant away. We had deemed it best that no one, except Mrs. Collins and Ward, should see him when he arrived. It was at Mr. Whitmore's request that I spent the night at Mr. Ward's house and the following morning Mr. Luckstone telephoned instructions to us.

"The fact that Mr. Whitmore took a pistol to the office with him leaves no doubt that he meant to make it appear he had committed suicide. He was a man of enormous vitality, but I suppose that once the spleen has been punctured it is only a question of hours when the strongest man must die! But I only surmise Mr. Whitmore's intentions from the facts of the case, for I never saw him alive after I left him in front of the opera house."

Beard sat down, wearied and worn from the strain of his recital. Miss Burden joined him and pressed a hand against his cheek. She did not repel the arm he slipped about her waist.

She did not repel the arm he put around her waist

Now that Beard had finished, everyone experienced a welcome sense of relief, as if a heavy burden had been lifted off their minds.

"I've come across many cases of wonderful nerve, but nothing to equal the pluck of that man Whitmore!" exclaimed Manning, unable to contain his growing admiration for the dead merchant.

"And he was one of the mildest-mannered men I ever met!" joined Beard.

The coroner, who had been making notes, now looked up at Britz. The detective's face had relaxed into an expression of mingled pity and contentment. Through the sorrow which the suffering of Mrs. Collins aroused in him, shone the satisfaction which he could not but feel at having finally squeezed all the mystery out of the Whitmore case.

"You believe Mr. Beard's statement, don't you?" the coroner inquired.

"I do."

"Then let us end this harrowing scene. I suppose my first duty is to discharge Mrs. Collins from custody?"

"There is no longer any reason for holding her," said Britz.

"As for Ward, I shall have to hold him for the formal inquest," the coroner announced.

"I don't believe he'll try to evade us," said Britz. "In view of all the circumstances I believe we're justified in permitting him to go on his own recognizance. Since Mr. Beard's story will undoubtedly be substantiated by the others, Ward's acquittal is a foregone conclusion. How soon can you hold the inquest?"

"I can impanel a coroner's jury to-morrow. But why this hurry?"

Britz shot a significant glance at Beard and Miss Burden. The secretary's arm was still about her waist.

"Beard, you'd better take out a marriage license at once," suggested Britz. "We're going to hold the inquest in this case to-morrow. You'll be called as the first witness and we'll finish with you as quickly as we can. There's a boat for Europe at two o'clock—it might be well for you and your bride to make it. You might as well be abroad while I wrestle with the Federal authorities to make them forget the substitution of prisoners."

www.ingramcontent.com/pod-product-compliance
Ingram Content Group UK Ltd.
Pitfield, Milton Keynes, MK11 3LW, UK
UKHW042149281224
453045UK00004B/253